Much Ado

About Vengeance

The Fair Hero Series

Book Two

Kerry Rockwood White

Cover photograph ©Dreamstime.com/Dundanim

KRW Designs Publications

Info@fairheroseries.com

ISBN-10: 0983592357

ISBN-13: 978-0-9835923-5-8

Printed in the United States of America

First Edition

14 13 12 11 10 / 10 9 8 7 6 5 4 3 2 1

To Aidan and Julia.

When you love to read, the

whole world is at your fingertips.

When you love to write, whole worlds

spring forth from your fingertips.

And here we go with the Thanks:

Don't get me wrong, I'm very happy to have people to thank. Without them, there'd be no book. I'm grateful that not only do I have people to thank, but that I have so many.

Thank you to Amy F. for all her love, support and editing assistance. Thank you to Wart and my little Spider Monkey for their friendship and laughter. Don't know what I'd do without you guys to keep me sane. Or insane. I can never figure out which. Hmm. That tells you something right there, doesn't it? Thank you to Kristina for not only getting me over my pedicure phobia (long story) but for being my first and most eager fan. Thank you to Heather, Nifer, Jessica, Michele, Donna and so many others that I just can't keep them all straight. Forgive me for not naming everyone – but I do my best to thank you guys on FB and you know who you are :) Thank you to all my IE peeps for their endless support. You guys are the best. A special thank you to Barbara V. for a correspondence that I will treasure all my life and for making me feel like a "real" author. Thank you to my family for all their love and support and for hocking my book! And thank you most of all to my husband, Dan, for standing by me through all the craziness and telling me to keep going. I love you.

NOTE: Since my husband just couldn't keep it straight while reading the story I figured I'd put a note here to help you out. The character introduced in this book is named Aton – pronounced Ah-tawn. Like Anton without the first "n". Also, because I've had some people ask, the character of Jaeger – his name is pronounced Yay-ger not Jay-ger. Hope that helps some of you :)

Chapter 1

Hello! Nice to see you again. I knew you'd be back! Well, I thought most of you would be back. Ok, I hoped some of you would be back. But look at you! You're all here! (Seriously, not all at once in the same place, what are you looking around for!?)

So, here we are for another round, another installment of the life of Hero Fletcher. I've got to tell you, I never thought there'd be a day when I'd be glad to consider the story of my life entertainment for the masses. But, we all do what we have to do to cope. With me, it's putting things down in black and white, otherwise I might be able to convince myself that some of these things never happened at all. And let me tell you, there are times, a lot of times, when that seems like such a great idea! But then that would leave too many inconvenient little holes in the fabric that covers the rest of my life. Which brings me back to you. The lucky, lucky people who get to read all about my trials and tribulations; who can ooh and ahh over the horrors from a safe distance, who can sympathize and empathize without having to be involved, and who can laugh at me without suffering the retaliation of my razor sharp, sarcastic wit.

And now you're thinking 'enough already, get on with it!' Ok, ok. Hold your horses. I just want to give a brief recap to those who are, for some reason, just joining us in book two without having first read book one. (And really, you should go and get book one immediately. You'll only be torturing yourself if you don't have it.)

For those who didn't read book one (yet), I am Hero Fletcher. Yes, that's my real name. My dad, an English lit professor, named me after a character in Shakespeare's *Much Ado About Nothing*. I have one sibling, William, who lives on the other side of the country. My dad lives in a neighboring state. My mom passed away and I live in her house, the house I grew up in. I have my own graphic design business, Hero Images. I've just turned 30, I have no children, have never been married (suppose that should have come first) and I am dating a vampire.

There. That about sums it up. Oh! I killed a woman named Leontine, who could shape shift into an orange cat. But it was self-defense. Actually, I'm still not 100% sure that I killed her and that it wasn't really Angel, a vampire pal, who finished her off. (Yes, I said a vampire named Angel. No, no relation.)

Alright then, I think we're good to go!

I was at home, admiring my new blender. I wasn't making anything in it. As a matter of fact, I couldn't recall that last time I'd made anything in the old one, but it was new and shiny and deserved to be admired.

"It's just a blender," Kin commented when I still hadn't joined him at the table.

"Yes, but's it's pretty. It's yellow. I've never had a yellow appliance before."

"Is yellow your favorite color?" he asked.

"No," I replied, "I just think yellow is pretty for kitchens."

2

"Well," Kin said, patting the table, "why don't you come and sit down and tell me what your favorite color is."

I smiled and turned obediently toward the kitchen table. "I bet I can guess yours," I said cockily. "You're a guy, so it's probably either red or blue." A smug smile stretched across my lips as I took the seat across from him.

"Wrong."

Damn! I hated being wrong. Even about something as trivial as favorite colors. Not willing to risk being wrong a second time so early in the day I said "So what is it then?"

"Actually, oddly enough, it's yellow."

"Oh, please! You're just saying that!"

Kin laughed that wonderful deep laugh that I had come to adore. "Truly, it is my favorite color. It's the color of sunshine."

Aw. Ok. Now what. Was I supposed to feel bad, laugh some more? I was at a loss. "Oh," I said inadequately. "So, it really is your favorite color?" Kin nodded. "Mine's green," I said matter-of-factly as I traced the pattern of the tablecloth with my index finger.

He gracefully rose out of his seat and slid himself across the table toward me. "Well, how lucky for me that I have green eyes?" he purred.

Hmm. I liked where this was going. "Yes, very lucky indeed," I replied, leaning in for a kiss. And you know what

3

came next. Oh, yeah. His damn cell phone rang! Sometimes I really hate modern technology, and this was one of those times.

Kin closed his eyes and sighed as he reached for his phone. Flipping it open, he settled back in his seat as he answered "McIntyre." Those lovely green eyes looked at me significantly and I knew that the Magistrate was on the other end of the line.

Darius was the Magistrate for the North East Sector. What exactly comprised the North East Sector I didn't know and frankly, I didn't care. I was just glad that there was some form of government and law and order among the undead. Of course, that didn't mean I was glad about Darius in other respects. On the contrary, I could live quite happily without ever seeing or hearing about Darius again.

My introduction into the vampiric world was less than stellar. After agreeing to hold onto an antique Russian snuff box for Kin that he'd purchased at an auction earlier that day, I found myself staring out my front window at a fanged freak. One hysterical call to the cops later, I had my house checked out and a police escort to a friend's house for the night. Fun, right? But wait, that's only the beginning. I returned home the next morning in the company of my good friend and a surly detective only to find my childhood home completely ransacked. Almost everything was destroyed (thus my pretty yellow blender). Then, my nice new boyfriend who had stuck me with the stupid snuff box tells me he's a vampire, the psycho outside my house was also a vampire and the bitchy blonde Amazon we ran into while obtaining the damn box was a vengeful shape-shifting cat-woman.

Uh huh. See? Told ya. Fun stuff. And 'cause all of this wasn't enough, Leontine (the cat-woman) was very sensitive and easily offended. Actually, I have to say a lot of the supernatural beings I've met so far have way too thin a skin. But she was actually offended just by the fact that I was a human! And she wanted to kill me. Lucky me. Which led to me being brought before Darius on a few occasions over a short period of time.

Let's just say that vampire or not, Darius is not the kind of guy you'd want to run into in a dark alley. He's not very tall, of course he's probably several hundred years old and men were shorter then. But despite his stature he is very intimidating. Very. He can sit behind his marble-topped desk, seemingly at ease, and without raising his voice or moving a muscle he can turn your blood cold with a few well-chosen words. Well, assuming you still have blood.

Kin flipped his phone shut and sighed. He sighed more than anyone I'd ever known. I was glad when I realized it wasn't just me that caused it. "Hero, I'm sorry, but..."

"Yeah, I know. You've got to go see Darius," I interrupted.

"Well, actually, yes," he fumbled, unsure how to say what needed to be said. "I, uh, have to go back for the last item I was, er, retrieving," he answered awkwardly.

"Oh!" Wow. Didn't see that coming. Just a couple of days before Kin had come home from a treasure hunt in some distant land that he wasn't allowed to tell me anything about. "I don't understand. Didn't you get the, the thing?" I'd had no idea what he had been after. Top secret vampire stuff.

"No. There were some customs issues and I left without it."

"Ohh! That can't be good. Wait, you're a vampire? How do you have customs issues? Can't you get around that stuff?"

"How? Hero, I can't turn into a bat and fly the thing back to the US. I've got to get on a plane like anyone else." I gave him a look that clearly indicated I reserved some doubts on the subject, but he continued. "Darius has ordered me to go back for it immediately."

I tried not to be sulky, but it was hard. He'd only just returned. "But you only just got back."

"I know," he said consolingly, brushing his fingertips against my cheek. "I'll try and get home as quickly as I can. I promise."

Then that annoying little warning bell went off in my head. "Wait a minute. What 'issues'?" I asked, not entirely sure I wanted to know.

"The antique business type of issues. Don't get yourself worried over nothing."

Damn! There he was again with his reasonable answers. Talk about annoying. Well, it wouldn't do any good to be sulky, so I smiled and tried to appear happy. Inside, I wanted to cry like a baby. But, I figured I'd be alone soon and could cry all I wanted then. "Easier said than done. I can't help worrying."

He got up and carried his half-empty bottle of Poland Springs to the fridge. "As I'm sure you can guess, Darius was less than happy that I came back empty-handed, but there was no way I was going to stay there. I had to see for myself that you were ok."

The reason Kin had left his top secret mission and returned to Massachusetts was because I'd called him frantically from our friend Hazel's house and told him to get me help. Hazel, a faerie friend I had been staying with, and Jaeger, a vampire hunter assigned to protect me, were under attack from Leontine and members of her menagerie. Being just a human surrounded by supernatural creatures, I was, naturally, terrified. I called Kin despite his being somewhere much too far away to help and basically ordered him to call Darius or someone and get help for me. It wasn't exactly the most thoughtful way to have done it but I was afraid for my life, so you've got to cut me some slack.

Needless to say, Kin got back home as quickly as he could, which I am sure did not please the Magistrate. I'd venture to guess that feelings for humans weren't running high at the Magistrate's mansion at the moment.

And now he had to go back again. And I couldn't help feeling it was my fault. Well, mostly my fault. Great, now I had guilt! I hate that. How was I supposed to wallow in feeling sorry for myself later when he was gone if I had to deal with guilt? Fortunately, guilt might affect the quality of my wallowing but it wouldn't affect the taste of Ben & Jerry's.

Chocolate! Thank you, God, for chocolate. Just the thought of never being able to eat chocolate again would be enough for me to want someone to stake me if I was a vampire. Oh, and that disgusting drinking blood part too. But no chocolate, why live? I've said it before and I'll say it again. It should be its own food group with a recommended daily allowance.

"So, I suppose you've got to go right away?"

"Yeah," he replied, as he came over and pulled me to my feet. "I wish I didn't have to though," he added as he finished the kiss we had started earlier. This time, it was my phone's turn to ring. Seriously, it's like a universal conspiracy.

"Ugh," I groaned as I went and picked up the receiver off the wall (yes, I still have a land line in addition to my cell phone). "Hello?"

"Hey, H! Whatchya doing?" asked my best friend Sue.

"Hey. I was just saying goodbye to Kin actually," I told her as I grinned ruefully at my handsome vampire boyfriend.

"Oh? Everything ok? You sound a little upset."

"Yeah, fine," I assured her. "He just has to go away on business for a little while." At least I hoped it was just a little while.

"Ah, got ya. Well, I'll let you two say your goodbyes then. But give me a call later, ok? We're trying to make plans for a New York theater weekend."

"Oh, cool! Sure, I'll give you a call later." I finished with Sue and told Kin about the possibility of a trip of my own.

"Sounds like fun," he said as he kissed me on the forehead. "When do I get to meet your friends?"

"You already met them at the bar the night we met. Remember?" I answered evasively, knowing full well that that was not going to suffice.

Predictably, he sighed. "Hero, you have a lot of very close friends. They're already upset over your house and you staying with me and then Hazel. If you keep me separate from them it's going to make it very hard for them to accept our relationship."

I knew he was right, but I was afraid. What if my friends realized something was different about Kin? Ok, not that anyone was going to say "Hey, you wouldn't happen to be a vampire, would you?" but they were bound to notice he doesn't eat and only takes the occasional sip of water. How was I going to explain that? How could I have him at our monthly get-togethers at TJ's? All we do is drink and eat and drink when we're there. Having to deal with all the traditional crap when you have a new boyfriend and a large, close-knit group of friends is bad enough, but this vampire stuff made it too much to deal with.

I came clean. "I'm just afraid of how to handle that you don't eat or drink. I mean, how do you have a gathering of a large group of people that doesn't involve food or drink? They're going to notice and I don't know how to explain that."

"Well, we could just say I am getting over a stomach flu." Wow! He certainly came up with that quick enough. Apparently, when you spend decades pretending not to be a vampire you're prepared him for such eventualities.

9

"Ok, but what about the next time? And the time after that?"

"We'll think of something, Hero. But you're going to have to have us together sooner or later if we're going to be a couple." Then he looked at me with those big green eyes. They were sad. Not fair. Worse than puppy eyes. I had a six-foot-something, well-built vampire in my kitchen looking at me with big, sad green eyes. So naturally, I did what any woman would do. I melted.

"Ok, we'll do something after you get back and you can blame your whatever-it-is on your traveling to some God-forsaken place."

"Terrific! Thanks, sweetheart," he said joyfully, emphasizing his glee with a hug and a kiss.

I laughed in spite of myself. I couldn't help it. "Ok, ok. The weather will be warming up soon. How about a cookout? Oh! Will that be ok?"

"Sure, I'll wear long sleeves and sunscreen. If the sun is strong that day I'll just stay in the shade. You've got some shady areas in your yard don't you?" he added hesitantly.

"Yeah, no problem. Debbie and Bob have a nice canopy thing I'm sure they'll let me borrow too."

And that was that. We had a plan. Well, the seeds of a plan. I still had to wait to find out when he'd be coming back home before I could really begin to make any solid plans. We embraced and kissed one last time before I walked him to the front door of my little house on Georgia Road.

"Thank you, Hero."

"Oh, enough already. It's no big deal."

"But it is," he said softly. "I know your friends are like your family and it means a lot to me that you are going to let me meet them." I shrugged self-consciously. I didn't want to get all mushy and sentimental. He was leaving after all.

"You be careful," I told him. "And call me when you can, even if you think it's late and I'd be asleep. Ok?"

"Ok, I promise. And I also promise to get home as quickly as I can so we can plan our barbeque."

I smiled at him. Hmm. Barbeque. "Oh! That reminds me! I'll have plenty of time to order sauce!"

"Order? Hero, there's a brand new bottle of barbeque sauce in your refrigerator. I was with you when you bought it two days ago."

"Pfft," I waved my hands at him. "That's ok for things like chicken nuggets and stuff. If we're having a cookout I've got to order some Cripple Creek! That cat-bitch poured mine out all over the floor when she trashed my house," I recalled bitterly. "Oh," I said a little disappointed. "Guess I'd better not get the roasted garlic."

"Uh, yeah. I would appreciate that."

"Caramelized onion ok?" He chuckled and nodded then I gave him one final kiss before he went out the door.

Gilbert O'Sullivan rang in my head. "Alone again, naturally." Well! That didn't take long. Kin hadn't even pulled out of the driveway and self-pity reared its ugly, chocolate-consuming head. Even the prospect of having an excuse to order my favorite gourmet barbeque sauce and host a cookout wasn't enough to deter me from a full-on wallow-fest.

I deserved to wallow, I told myself. After all, only a few days before I had been hiding out in the house of a faerie where we had come under attack from vampires and shape shifters. I'd had to fight for my life against an angry blonde Sasquatch who was much stronger that I am and was doing a great job of beating the crap out of me.

Fortunately for me, despite all the babble and sarcasm that comes out of my mouth and rambles around in my head, sometimes I can be a very rational and logical person. Don't laugh, it happens. I'd had the forethought to put a letter opener I had found in the desk into my pants pocket before Leontine had gotten into the house. During my beating, I had a rare moment of clarity where I was able to startle my enemy and jab the letter opener into her neck. The rest is gory and messy and you can pretty much guess it if you haven't read the first book (and if you haven't, why not?), so I won't go on.

But needless to say, I was a mess. I was in pain. I was bruised inside and out. After being forced to stay at Darius' mansion until Kin returned, I finally got to go home to a nearly empty house that had only had a couple of necessities replaced. It was like being assaulted all over again. So Kin took me shopping for other things to try and make me feel better and more at home. Just a loan, of course, until my insurance check arrives. I'm not one of those women who let men buy her stuff.

But now he was gone again. And I was alone again. And even though it was my home, it wasn't. Everything was new and strange. Except for most of the things in my office and a few larger pieces of furniture in the kitchen and the dining room, which I rarely used, it was all new.

I sat on my lovely new couch and stared out the front windows. My lovely oatmeal and brown flecked couch that matched the fabulous arm chair with the retro patterned upholstery and the little wooden legs. And the darling burnt-orange chaise that matched the boomerang shape in the pattern on the chair. All the pieces coordinated so well with each other and the new tables and lamps and carpet. But they were strangers here.

Mom. Mom had never sat on this furniture. She'd never scolded me for putting my feet on this coffee table. She wasn't here to give me grief over buying a sofa with pale colored fabric. "It will show everything!" she would have cautioned. What I wouldn't give to be reproached by her now.

Snuffling in a most unbecoming fashion, I turned on the TV and flipped to the Lifetime Movie Network. I was in the mood for a cry, and since this channel was aptly nicknamed the "Tears and Tissues Network" by several of the male members of my group, it was the obvious choice. Then I went to the kitchen to liberate some Ben & Jerry's from the cold recesses of the freezer. I grabbed a spoon, some napkins, tissues, a can of Diet Sprite, a bottle of Excederin, and I was ready. Pity train ready to depart!

Chapter 2

Is it possible to have a chocolate hangover? Because I think I've had one. A whole pint of New York Super Fudge Chunk, two packs of Ring Dings and a lovely box of assorted chocolate Pepperidge Farm cookies shouldn't have done me any damage; I have a high chocolate tolerance. But perhaps all of that combined with crying out of self-pity and crying over Steel Magnolias for the ten thousandth time had me feeling like my head had been filled with concrete and then jackhammered back to dust. It was also very, very wrong that an evening dedicated to chocolate should leave my mouth tasting and feeling the way it did. I'll spare you those grisly details. Some of you may be eating.

Well, there was only one thing to be done; a little hair of the dog. So I trudged to the kitchen and grabbed a glass. Then I got the milk and the Oreos and went to my computer. I dunked and chomped and slurped while I checked my email, the crisp, dark chocolate and the cold, rich milk restoring my taste buds and soothing my aching head. Don't judge me. You recover your way, I'll recover mine.

I needed to snap out of my funk or I'd spend the day feeling sorry for myself and I couldn't afford a marathon binge. Kin would be coming home to a much larger girlfriend and I'd have to buy new jeans. So, I steeled myself and picked up the phone. I couldn't let Sue know I was feeling down.

"Hey, Sue," I said when she answered. "Sorry. I did call you back last night but I got your voicemail and I was going to call again but I fell asleep watching TV."

"Hi, hun. Yeah, I saw that I missed your call. No biggie. I was talking to Carol and Jenn and they wanted to make plans for another theater weekend. You in?"

"Sure! What are we going to see?" I asked with more enthusiasm than I really felt.

"Well, we've got votes for Million Dollar Quartet, Memphis and The Addams Family."

"Ooh! Million Dollar Quartet! I'd love to see that. And you know, I'll always see Wicked again."

Sue laughed. "Again! You've seen it three times!"

"I know, but it's good!" Ow! The smiling hurt my head.

"You're not fooling anyone. You just want an excuse to sing "Popular".

"I have no idea what you're talking about. I'll sing whatever I want to sing whenever I want to sing it. I don't need an excuse," I defended.

She laughed again. "That's true! We're thinking the last weekend in July. Will that work for you?"

Would it? I flipped to my calendar. As far as I knew it was open, but Kin wasn't around for me to ask. Not that

15

he'd tell me not to go, but it seemed a bit rude not to clear it with him. "Yeah, that's fine," I told her, making an executive decision. After all, he could be sent away again at any moment so I might as well go ahead and make my own plans.

As though she had been reading my mind, Sue asked "Do you need to check that with Kin?"

"No, it'll be fine."

"Uh-huh. Things not going so well?"

"What? No! Things are fine! Why would you say that?"

"Because you didn't need to check it with him. Normally couples do that, especially at the beginning when they're all lovey-dovey and sickening and all that," she explained, barely disguising her distaste.

"You sentimental fool. I don't need to check with Kin because his business requires him to travel at a moment's notice, so he won't object to me making my own plans. And thank you for making me feel so great about what I was going to ask you!"

"Oh, crap. What have I done now?"

"Well, Kin is actually travelling for, uh, business now, but when he gets back I want to have a cookout so everyone can meet him."

"Oh! Well, what's wrong with that?" she said relieved.

"Nothing's wrong with it, but after the lovey-dovey comment I figured you wouldn't want to come."

"No! I think it's great. And everybody wants to meet this guy. If you hadn't met him in front of us, people would be doubting whether he was even real." Sue said this with a chuckle, but in my stomach I had a sick feeling. All I could think was if she had said "whether he was even human." Of course, why in the world would she say that, but even so, the idea still popped right into my throbbing head.

"Of course he's real! Like I'd make up a boyfriend! My God! Would you guys really think I'd be so pathetic that I'd make up a boyfriend?" Ok, bad idea. Not that I didn't have an excellent point and every right to be irate, but holy crap that mini rant made my skull feel like it was about to shatter into a million pieces.

"Chill out, H. You know I was just joking. I think the cookout is a great idea. You let me know when it's going to be and what I can bring, ok?"

"Ok," I agreed petulantly. "Let me know about New York and how much I'll owe you and all that."

"Will do. Talk to you later, hun."

I said good-bye and hung up the phone. Well, that might have cleared an obligation off my list but it did nothing for my pounding head or my mood.

Determined to get the better of my chocolate hangover and my self-pity, I absorbed myself in my work. I had a customer who wanted a new logo for their jewelry business,

17

in addition to letterhead and other stationery needs. It was fairly simple and straightforward design work, but it gave me something else to focus on. Plus, I had to admit, I liked looking at the pictures of all the handmade jewelry on their website.

A few hours later, samples sent to the client for approval, I was feeling something more recognizable as myself. I went out the kitchen, rinsed the empty glass, the empty milk carton and put the Oreos away. Ok, what was left of the Oreos. I made myself a cup of tea while I contemplated lunch. Breakfast being what it was, I decided I needed a very healthy lunch.

After a quick perusal of my freezer, I opted for a medley of Mediterranean vegetables with rice and barley. Not as tempting as dark chocolate and cream, I grant you, but appetizing none-the-less. Box opened, tray vented and popped into the microwave, I stood and waited for the beep.

Where was Kin? Was he in another country? Was he in danger? Or worse! Was he with some gorgeous woman! Hmm. Where did that come from? Jealousy. That was new. This separation might require more than chocolate. I know, I know. Shocking to think that chocolate is not enough.

The microwave beeped and I took out my entree and stirred it before returning it to the oven. I didn't like that momentary lapse. It wasn't like me at all. This called for Girl Power. As soon as I returned to my office I sent out the BAT signal, which in our little gaggle of geese stands for Bitching and Tears. It's our call to arms when one of us is feeling down or needs the moral support of her sister friends.

Naturally, replies came fast and furious and in a matter of minutes plans were made for a hen's only dinner at TJ's, our local hangout. The overwhelming and immediate response of my friends helped enormously. I started to feel better. After the events of the past couple of weeks, this was just what I needed.

A shower completed my resurrection and I was looking my old self when I walked into TJ's at the appointed hour. Since it was just us girls I had pulled my dark brown hair back into a clip at my nape and was wearing a comfy, yet well fitting, pair of jeans with a red gingham baby doll top and my white tennis sneakers. I wasn't looking to impress anyone, and I like my tennis sneakers.

Jennifer and Amy were already there and had a large basket of fries in the middle of the table. I pulled up a chair and signaled to the waitress. "Hey, guys."

"Hey, yourself! You ok, hun?" Amy asked, obviously concerned.

"Oh, yeah. Just feeling sorry for myself. My house, Mom."

"I know. That sucks! Have they found out who did it yet?"

"No, Jenn, not yet." I hated lying, but I couldn't tell them a psycho blonde who could change into an orange cat trashed my house because she hated humans.

"I don't know how you feel safe there on your own." The silence at the table spoke volumes. "Oh my gosh! I'm sorry, H! I just meant, you must feel uncomfortable there with whoever did it still out there."

"Yes, well, since you put it that way, that's much better," I replied sarcastically. "Don't worry about it, Amy," I told her, holding up a hand, when I saw her turn an even deeper shade of red and open her mouth to try and explain again. "I know what you meant and that you said it out of concern. I really do. I've had an alarm installed so I'm ok there alone, honest."

"Sorry," she whispered anyway. I winked at her to show it was all ok. The waitress brought my rum and coke and asked my pals if they were ready for another round.

"Yes, please," answered Jennifer. "And I think we can order some food now. The others should be here any time now."

As if on cue, Carol strolled through the door and Sue and Debbie came in right behind her. Various pizzas and appetizers were ordered along with cocktails. This was Ladies' Night. No pitchers of beer this evening.

Before long the whole gang was there and I was duly put on the spot. Time to 'fess up, Hero. Don't you just hate that? You want your friends around you, you want support, you're feeling down, feeling blue, and what happens? They make you spill your guts, and in public too. Yeah, yeah, I know. They're owed an explanation, after all, I raised the BAT signal, but my troubles should be revealed organically as the night unfolds. It shouldn't be the Spanish Inquisition.

I steeled myself for the onslaught. "What did he do? What did he say? Did he hurt you? Blah, blah, blah." Ok, I know I sound like an ungrateful bitch. I'm not looking too good in black and white here. But honestly, put yourself in my position. I rallied to troops to cheer me up and help me feel better and they're putting me on the spot and assuming the worst of Kin when he hasn't done anything at all. Well, fine, yeah he's a vampire, but he didn't exactly have a choice in the matter. Can't hold that against him. Ugh! Or would they? There we go. There it was, the heart of the problem. 'Ok, ladies, I'll tell you what's really bothering me. You see I'm dating a vampire and I just don't know how all of you are going to take it.' Even saying it in my head made me feel sick.

"Guys, guys, GUYS!" I yelled over the clamor. "You guys are awesome, thank you so much for being here for me. I really needed to be with my girlfriends tonight. Kin got sent away on business again on a moment's notice and I'm in a house full of strange stuff and missing memories, and it's just… it's just hard. It hit me hard all at once. I had to get out and be with you guys."

A chorus of 'aws' and 'ohs' followed by hugs and protestations of love and fidelity ensued and everyone was satisfied. Everyone except me. I know, you're stunned!

That little voice in my head that kept saying 'what the hell have you gotten yourself into now, Hero?' was more persistent that ever. I was in love with a vampire. I had to find a way for my vampire boyfriend to interact with my normal friends. And not just interact, but I had the absolutely brilliant scheme of planning a barbeque! Sometimes I wondered if Leontine didn't bash a few of my brain cells to death! Yes, a barbeque where everyone will be consuming huge quantities of food and drink, except for my boyfriend, who will already be under the microscope. Oh, and while we're at it, let's have a houseful of people remarking on all my new stuff and all the stuff that's gone and different and reminding me constantly of what I've lost. "Lucy!" I bellowed, signaling the waitress. "Bring me an Alabama Slammer. Or three."

While I wallowed in the misery of my life I watched my friends dancing and joking and laughing. They were wonderful. I was really lucky after all. I couldn't help smiling while they all sang along at the tops of their lungs to "Love Shack", most of them on the floor dancing, the others dancing in their seats. What a wonderful, wacky bunch of idiots. And here I was, The Mistress of Gloom. Ok, then. Enough was enough. I'd wallowed plenty. It was time to enjoy myself and stop worrying about what I couldn't change. I ran up onto the dance floor and jumped and spun around with Sue and Debbie and Jennifer and the others. It felt great!

When it was over they played "Magic" by the Cars and I had an epiphany. Duh! I nearly slapped my own head, but caught myself. Would've been fun explaining that one. Wonder if the old 'I could've had a V8' would've worked? Probably, we'd had enough to drink. Magic. Hazel! I'd call Hazel! Surely she could think of something that could help me. Instantly I felt relieved. The weight of the world no longer rested upon my shoulders.

"What are you so happy about?" Amy asked, seeing the euphoric look upon my face.

"Oh, I just love this song."

Chapter 3

Is it just me or do you ever feel like God is just sitting up there waiting to mess with you? Like He's got you on His schedule or something. 'What's on the agenda for today Peter?' 'Well, God, you're screwing up Hero Fletcher's life again at noon.' 'Excellent, I just love messing with her!' Because I have to tell you, I wouldn't be at all surprised. I know what some of you are thinking, God's got more important things to do. Well of course he does, but He's God! Don't you think He needs to unwind and kickback? What do you suppose He does for fun?

Alright, maybe not. Maybe it's just a spur of the moment thing with Him. I don't know, but I know He likes messing with me. If you agree, let me know. It'd be nice to know I'm not alone in this.

So why, you ask, am I so full of cosmic conspiracy theories? Because last night I thought I'd found an answer to my problem. Hazel, remember? Ok, good.

Well, it turns out not so good. I woke up this morning to sirens blaring all over the place. Just what I needed after a night of drinking. I looked out the window and there'd been a huge accident up on the corner of the block. Looked pretty bad too. How I didn't hear the accident itself I'll never know, but I was grateful for those few extra moments of sleep. I got up, got dressed, yadda, yadda. Went and found out what was going on. Couple of cars, speeding, young kids, hurt but didn't look too serious, thankfully. But power and landlines were out temporarily. Great! No work.

Wait, it gets better. I grabbed something to eat, brushed my teeth and, well, did what you do in the bathroom. And then... as I stood up to pull myself together, I flushed my cell phone down the toilet. Oh yeah, no need to reread that passage. You got it right the first time. I flushed my cell phone. Right down. All the way down. Note to self: When you replace said cell phone get one of those big honking monstrosities that will get stuck and NOT FIT down the drain!

So, how is your day going? It's ok, I'll wait until you're done laughing at me.......

Yeah, ok, enough. Moving on. No land line, no cell phone, no internet. Can't get out of my driveway because it's blocked by emergency vehicles. Naturally, my mind went where any reasonable person's would. To chocolate. But between my binge the other day and my night of drinking, I resisted. For now. Besides it was still early, and if this was how my day was starting, I may have a desperate need for that chocolate later and I'd hate to deplete the stores.

With nothing else to occupy me, I relented and went and stood outside with the neighbors. At least they could report back to my father that they'd seen me and I was well. "Hey, Mr. Blansett," I called to my next door neighbor.

"Hero, how are you?" he asked, genuinely interested. He was a nice old man who had lived next door for as long as I could remember.

"I'm doing fine, sir, thank you. How about you?"

"Good, good. Awful thing, this, huh? Damn kids, driving too fast."

"Is that what happened?" I replied, having just come out into the thick of things.

"Yeah. They were trying to beat each other to Nantasket," he said.

"Nantasket!" I said surprised. "That's still quite a way to go from here."

Mr. Blansett just nodded at me. "Summer hasn't even begun and they'll spend it in casts."

It may not have been the nicest reaction in the world, but I couldn't help feeling a brief moment of gratitude for the reminder that sometimes God screws with other people too. And sometimes worse than me. Although just using my bathroom is hardly on par with racing another teen to a beach that was still a good 20 minutes away.

The tow trucks finally secured their loads and departed. A fireman swept the glass from the street and the police and the neighbors went back to their business. I said goodbye to Mr. Blansett and went inside to see if I could call Hazel.

Just to prove me wrong, God had the phone line already fixed. (Yes, I can make anything about me if I try hard enough. It's a gift.) So, I quickly dialed Hazel's number and asked her if she would come over and see me. Naturally, being such a sweet person, er um, faerie, Hazel said she'd come right over.

I went into the kitchen and poured a couple of glasses of iced tea and placed them on a tray with a plate of assorted cookies. Hazel appreciates thoughtful little gestures like that. Then I went into the living room to wait for her.

Let me rephrase. I went into the living room to meet Hazel. She was already sitting in my living room. "Ah!" I exclaimed as I nearly jumped out of my skin. "Hazel! I didn't expect you to be here, inside."

"Well, you asked if I could come right over so I thought it best to use magic rather than drive, and I didn't think you'd want me to risk any of your neighbors seeing me just suddenly appear on your front lawn," she stated quite calmly and rationally. Have I ever mentioned how much I hate calm and rational unless I'm the one being calm and rational? No? Well, I've mentioned it now. Make note.

I took a deep steadying breath and sat down next to her on the sofa. "Ok, I understand. Thanks for coming so quickly."

"Of course, Hero. Now what it is, what's happened, dear? You aren't in any trouble, I hope?"

"Me? Oh! No, I'm fine. Well, sort of." I quickly told her about the phone/phone/computer situation. To her credit, she barely smirked when I told her about flushing my cell.

"Mmm hmm," was her only response. I suspected she was trying not to laugh. I appreciated the effort.

"But luckily, the landline is working again. Don't know what I'm going to do about my cell. How do you explain that to a plumber?"

"Ha!" she couldn't hold it in any longer. The image of me trying to explain to a plumber how I managed to flush my cell phone was too much. "Hero, leave that to me, ok?"

"You know a good plumber?"

More laughter. At my expense. Just what I needed. "No! I mean I'll retrieve your phone for you!"

"Did you hear the part about it being flushed down the toilet," I reminded her.

"Yes, but I can use magic to get it out. And also to fix it and clean it," she added quickly, "so don't worry."

"I'm sorry, Hazel. I didn't realize. I'm sort of discombobulated this morning."

The red-haired faerie accepted my apology but she remained amused. "So, what was it you needed, Hero? You didn't call me just to get your cell phone back?"

"Oh! The reason I called you was I hoping there was some way you could help me with Kin and my friends."

"What do you mean?" she asked, shaking her head in confusion.

I explained about the upcoming cookout and my fears and concerns about having Kin around my friends. Hazel just blinked at me. "This was your emergency?"

"Oh!" I started, taken aback. "I didn't realize I said it was an emergency. I thought I just said I needed your help with something. I'm sorry if I gave you the wrong idea."

"Hero, you are dating a vampire. You are not a vampire. Your friends are not vampires. Sooner or later something will have to give. That's what happens when you date outside your species."

Wow! So not the attitude I was expecting from Hazel, my little cocktail-making faerie friend. "So, you... Hazel, I thought you and Kin were friends?"

"We are. But that doesn't mean you don't have to face the reality of the fact that you are dating a vampire."

"Believe me, I am! I just want my friends to have a chance to get to know him, without noticing the things that might otherwise make him seem weird. Why is that so much to ask?"

"Is that what you're really asking? Because I think what you really want is a way to hide the fact that your boyfriend is a vampire forever."

"Well, so what if I do? Do you really expect all my friends just to take it in stride that vampires are real and that I happen to be dating one? Come on, Hazel! They will freak out! They'll want to kill him, or commit me, or both! Maybe in this case ignorance really is bliss."

"Do you plan on telling anyone?" To be honest, I hadn't, and I said so. "Then it sounds to me like you want to pretend he's not really a vampire either, Hero. Hang on," she said as she flitted out of the room.

I didn't know where she was going or what she was doing. This was not the conversation I had been expecting to have. I had hoped Hazel would be able to put some sort of enchantment on the house so that my friends would just not notice how much Kin ate or drank on the day of the cookout. I didn't know how enchantments worked but compared to some I'd heard about, that one didn't sound too complicated to me.

My heart was hammering in my chest. I didn't like what she had said. Was I trying to pretend Kin wasn't really a vampire? I hadn't thought so. I was aware of it. I tried not to think about the unpleasant side of it, when he fed and things like that. Most of the time I just thought of Kin as Kin.

Hazel reappeared silently and handed me my cell phone. I hesitated a moment before taking it. It looked clean and dry. "Thank you," I told her.

"You're welcome. It should work just fine."

"Thank you."

Hazel nodded again. I didn't like her being upset with me. It wasn't like Hazel.

"Hazel, please sit down. I could get us some more tea. We can talk about other things. Please?" She wanted to stay mad but she couldn't. She smiled and sat down.

"No tea, thank you, but I'll stay a bit longer. Other than your worries over your cookout, how are you?" she asked.

I shrugged. "I'm ok, I guess. Getting used to my home being different. It feels strange."

We talked for several minutes then quite unexpectedly Hazel stood up and reached into her bag of stones. "I have to go, Hero, I'm sorry. I wish I could help you, but I think you need to work on this one yourself. If Kin is going to be a part of your life, you have to find a way of making him fit in. You can't rely on magic."

Sighing heavily, I stood to hug her good-bye. "Thank you, Hazel. I understand, and it's good advice. Thanks for the phone." After giving each other a kiss on the cheek, the faerie with the shocking red hair slowly dissolved out of my living room.

Immediately I headed for the kitchen. Ring Dings to the rescue! See, I knew I was going to need chocolate later. I had hoped much later, but the point was, I needed it and it was here.

I looked down at my cell phone. It looked ok. I risked a sniff. Nope, still smelled like a cell phone, and nothing else. I checked to see if I had missed any calls or messages since the sinking. Just one from my service provider. Big deal.

Against my better judgment, I dialed Kin's number. To my surprise and delight he picked up on the second ring! "Hero! Are you developing a sixth sense?" he asked, his voice full of laughter. Oh, boy! I needed to hear that.

"No, why?"

"I was just going to call you!"

"Really?" I exclaimed, not bothering to hide my shock.

"Yes," he laughed, "I really was. I'm lucky enough to be in a spot that gets decent reception at the moment so I was going to call."

We chatted for a few minutes. Useless, senseless babble. The inane banter that passes as conversation between two people who really have nothing to say but want very much to hear each other's voices.

"So, how long is it going to take you to clear up this customs stuff?"

"I really don't know. The funny thing is, the item isn't even native to them and they know it."

"Do you think they know what it is?"

"No, I doubt that. Humans aren't interested in the text."

"Well, not that you know of."

He laughed at me then. I wasn't crazy about it. It was meant as playful and harmless, but it pissed me off just the same. I tried not to let it show.

"Don't be silly, Hero! Very, very few humans have any idea of its existence and it's of no use to them. Hopefully I'll be home within the week. I'll have to go see Darius first thing when I get in, of course, but I'll call you as soon as I'm through. Ok?"

"Ok! Have a safe trip."

We said our good-byes and I hung up the phone. Maybe it was just stubbornness on my part, and maybe not, but if he'd told me about the text or whatever the hell it was, how many other humans had been told over the centuries? And how many humans had *they* told? Perhaps I was just sticking up for my species, but I didn't think he should be discounting the human race so quickly.

What was this damned text thing anyway? They wouldn't even call it by its real name. Why? Was it that sensitive or were they? I couldn't help wondering, and not for the first time, if this wasn't some elaborate goose chase. It made no sense.

If there were some ancient text that was super important to vampires and other supernatural beings, why would Grigoryi Aleksey Sereysky have hidden it in the first place? Why not use it? Or at least given it to some other vampire who could use it responsibly? If it couldn't be used responsibly, then why not destroy it? And what the hell was up with the stupid puzzle hidden in the hallmarks on the back of his silver products that have been scattered all over the world? Maybe it's because I'm not a vampire, but not the brightest idea, in my opinion.

And what is the freaking thing supposed to do anyway? I'll be honest, that's what I really wanted to know. What made it worth all these centuries of searching and made it worth ol' Grigsy meeting his true death?

I don't about you, but when you see those scenes in movies and TV where they torture people to find out where some item is hidden, I can't think of anything in my life I'd be willing to withstand that kind of crap to hide, can you? Nope. I love Kin, but if someone wanted to break my hands, cut off fingers, burn me with cigars, and on and on, I'd give him up as a vampire pretty damn quick. He's a big boy, he can take care of himself. And other than that and my real weight, what do I have to hide?

Think about it. After all Grigoryi sacrificed, he still had no idea which vampire(s) or what kind of supernatural being would ultimately find the text (whatever the hell it is) and what they would use it for. He could have chosen to live and do whatever he could do to stop or counteract the vamp that was after the text. Personally, I would have given it up. But that's me. If that makes me a coward, I can live with that. The operative word being 'live'.

Speaking of live, how am I supposed to live with a vampire boyfriend amid a life full of normal people? If Oprah did a show on this, I missed it.

I did understand where Hazel was coming from, even though I was still just a little bit hurt that she couldn't see my point of view. I truly wasn't thinking about her putting a charm or spell or whatever on my friends forever. I had only wanted it for the cookout so they could get a chance to know Kin before I started.... Started what? Telling them he was a vampire?

Uuuuuugggghhhh! I flopped myself down on the chaise in my best dramatic flop. Maybe Hazel was more right than I realized. Maybe that's what really hurt. I don't know, this was still uncharted territory for me. I guess once I had used her magic to get by and avoid telling people the truth it would make it too tempting to keep going to the well. After all, it's not like I didn't really want to avoid having to tell the truth. I did. I wanted to big time. I wanted to avoid it more than I wanted to avoid telling my parents how I managed to submerge their car in the Dorgan's pool (long story).

Even if they liked Kin, how was I going to broach the subject? 'Hey, that's great! So glad that you like him. By the way, did I happen to mention he's a vampire?' Obviously that was out. 'Yes, his work is very interesting. Oh, he doesn't mind all the traveling and long hours at all. Vampires never mind that sort of thing. What? I didn't mention he was a vampire?' Mmm, no that wouldn't do it. How about a more direct approach? 'Now, I know you're not going to believe this, but it's time for me to tell you the truth. Kin is a vampire.' Yeah, right. Dr. Freud on line one for you, Hero.

Even if they meet and like him first, there's still no easy way to tell them. Damn it! I wish vampires really could do that glamor thing and I'd just have him take them into the house one at a time and tell them himself. Coward! How like me, to want to make him tell them himself. I hated to admit it, but I loved the sound of that. Ok, ok – calm down! I'm not going to ask him to do it! I know I've got to be the one, but that doesn't mean I can't think about how much I'd rather pass it off onto him. I mean, he is the one who's the vampire, you know? It is his news to tell when you think about it.

Maybe a cookout wasn't the best idea after all. Maybe it would be better to meet my friends in pairs. Double date. Movies. Yeah! He could pretend to be sharing the popcorn with me and not be hungry afterward. Then I could confide in one friend at a time and tell them it was a secret and not to tell anybody else. Once I'd gone through everybody and they all knew, I could let them know it was out of the bag. My God, I really was a coward. When did that happen? Duh! When I started dating a vampire, of course.

I got up and carried the tray of empty iced tea glasses and cookies out to the kitchen. After washing up the glasses and putting things away, I stood at the back door and tried to imagine my future cookout. No matter how I pictured it, it didn't end well. I hated being pessimistic; it wasn't my natural state.

As I turned to go back in and shut the door, I saw a shadow out of the corner of my eye at the edge of the yard. I closed my eyes and rested my head against the door jam. "No, no, no, no," I muttered to myself. "Not this shit again!"

Carefully, I raised one eyelid just a crack to see if I could catch sight of anyone, or anything, lurking in my back yard. There didn't appear to be anything out of the ordinary going on, but, in the past few weeks I'd learned that that meant nothing.

I closed the door and bolted it and set the security alarm. Then I went and double checked the front door and the windows. Once things were secure, I sat down on the bottom of the steps in the hallway.

"Ok, Hero," I said to myself, "you're just imagining things. It's probably just a branch moving or a cat." Ew! That didn't help. I'd never like cats again as long as I lived. Not their fault, but you really can't blame me for that one.

Reminding myself once again how I had sworn to cut down the hedge that ran along the side of my property, I crept to the front window and peered out into the driveway as the first shadows of twilight began to stretch out over my front lawn.

I lifted up the corner of the curtain and I scanned the area for a sign of anything out of the ordinary. Ha! I almost laughed out loud at that. Out of the ordinary. My whole world had become out of the ordinary in the past few weeks. I reeled in the laughter and focused on the exterior of the house. It occurred to me that if anyone could see me now, crouched down on the floor, peeking out of the corner of my window with the curtain resting on my head, they might think I'd lost it. Sighing, I let go of the curtain and straightened up. If it was a vampire, it wasn't coming in without an invitation. If it was just some wacko, I had my alarm system. If it was something else.... Well, I didn't know, but I had no idea why 'a something else' would be out there watching me. At least, not this time.

I ran my hands through my hair. What the hell was happening to my life? Returning to the kitchen, I made myself something to eat, grabbed the remains of the Oreos and a drink and headed upstairs. Perhaps Steven King wasn't the wisest choice of authors to read under such circumstances, but I was already into the book. I got comfortable and ate and immersed myself in the book, trying to forget that niggling sense that someone or something was out there watching me. Again.

Chapter 4

Ok, so, let's add things up. A chocolate hangover (unheard of in my universe), flushing my cell phone, and now, a vivid and horrible nightmare where I was being stalked by giant Oreos out for revenge for all the Oreos I've drown and consumed in my lifetime. Don't you dare tell me that God doesn't like screwing with me.

Wait! I nearly forgot! The cherry on the cake! The lovely big bump I have on my forehead thanks to falling out of the bed and into my nightstand while trying to wrangle myself free from the grip of a very angry Double Stuff.

I spent the day submerged in my work, trying desperately not to think about anything else. I'm sure you can all guess how that worked out. When a knock came on the front door in the afternoon I actually screamed and jumped out of my chair. Another stellar moment to add to the growing list of weekly embarrassments.

With my faerie-retrieved cell phone in hand, ready to dial 911 if needed, I went to the front door and called out "Who is it?" Wow, how lame was that? Especially since I have a peephole and could have looked, but that would have meant touching the door.

"Hey, Hero. It's Mike. You know, Mike Avery, Kin's friend?"

Well, that was certainly unexpected. I opened the door. "Hi, Mike. How are you?" I asked hoping I didn't seem too surprised.

"Oh, I'm doing ok, thanks, Hero. I just thought I'd stop by and say 'hi'." Then he added in a whisper, "You know, with Kin being away and all, I thought maybe he'd like it if I checked on you."

Aw, how cute was that? "I'm sure he'd really appreciate it. Come on in, Mike" I said opening the door all the way so he could enter.

"Oh!" he said looking shocked. "No, I wasn't trying to get myself invited in or nothing like that, honest. I was just trying to make sure you was ok."

I had to struggle not to laugh. "Mike, it's ok. Really, I'd like the company. It would be nice to visit with you for a few minutes. That is, if you have the time."

He hesitated. I could see he was torn. Poor Mike didn't know if it would be rude to say no and not accept my invitation or if it would be offensive to Kin and go and spend time with his girlfriend in his absence.

I decided to help him out. "You are my friend too, aren't you, Mike?"

He gave a little gasp. "Oh, of course, Hero. Sure, sure. We're friends."

"Great! Then there's no reason why my friend Mike can't come on in for a few minutes to let me know how he's doing.

I know Kin would think it was great that we were becoming good friends."

That seemed to perk him up a bit. "Well, if you think it'd be alright."

That did the trick. In came my vampire visitor. I liked Mike. He was a sweet kid, even if he was a vampire. He hadn't been one long enough to shed all his human qualities. When I had been staying at the Magistrate's mansion just a few days earlier, Mike had confided in me that he was having a hard time adjusting to the undead life.

He came and sat in my living room and we chatted about the weather, the Red Sox, my new furniture and a funny story Mike had about an argument between two vampires at the mansion the night before. Apparently, one vampire had fed off the girlfriend of another vampire, without his permission. (Seems to me what really mattered was whether he had *her* permission, but what do I know about such things?) But the vampire with the girlfriend was claiming it was revenge for stealing a woman away from the first vampire over a hundred years ago. Seriously? Talk about holding a grudge! One hundred years. I wanted to ask if their names were Hatfield and McCoy, but something told me Mike wouldn't get it.

Oh, and yes, I know that story didn't seem funny, but it's a vampire thing. If you heard Mike tell it and how they behaved to one another and the attitudes of the other vampires in the antechamber, it was funny. Not hysterical, but funny. Trust me on this one.

I felt awkward because I couldn't really offer him anything and I was getting hungry. When my stomach loudly protested my negligence, Mike couldn't help but hear it, even if he hadn't had super vampire hearing.

"Aw geez, I'm sorry, Hero. I'm probably keeping you from your supper, huh? I forget about stuff like that now."

"Don't worry about it, Mike. It was nice talking to you." I walked him to the door, assuring him that it was fine that he had come and even more fine that he had come inside to visit.

As I opened the front door, I couldn't help but notice Mike scan the front yard. Oh oh! Danger, danger, danger!!!! The robot warning was screaming in my head. "What is it, Mike?" I whispered, never taking my eyes off of him.

He started to deny anything, but I stopped him with a small shake of my head. "It's ok, Mike. I'm safer if you tell me the truth. Honest. I saw your look. Just pretend we're still talking and everything is ok. Tell me what's really going on."

Mike looked even more nervous now. Not a good poker player. "I wish I could, Hero. Honest, I do. I'm not even sure myself. I just," he paused to gulp. "I just had a strange feeling that something wasn't right, so I came to check on you."

"Thank you, Mike," I answered, trying to remain calm. Believe me, it wasn't easy. "Can you tell me what made you feel like you should check on me?"

Shaking his head, Mike started to go out the door. "I shouldn'ta said nothing. You just go back inside, Hero, ok?"

"Please, Mike. If you were worried enough to have to come here, then I should know what's going on."

He swiveled his head all around, frantically searching every inch of my yard and the areas beyond. "I told ya, I don't even know nothing. It was just a feeling."

I reached out and took his hand. "What was this feeling based on, Mike? What happened to give you this feeling?" I was pleading with him now.

Leaning in close, Mike whispered, "I heard Darius telling Jaeger to keep an eye on you."

"What?!" I exclaimed. And like a frightened rabbit, Mike was gone in an instant, his vampire super speed carrying him away before I could draw another breath.

Holy crap! It was déjà vu! Didn't I just wake up from this nightmare last week? I rubbed my hands over my face, bracing myself for the reality of this new level of hell.

"Jaeger! Jaeger, come out and talk to me! I know you told me not to do this again, but if you come on my property you have to play by my rules."

Nothing. I walked back inside, leaving the front door open. I grabbed a pack of blueberry Pop Tarts and a bottle of water and went back outside. There I settled down on the front stoop and waited for Jaeger to show himself. Now, I'm sure what some of you are thinking but I'd spent too much time recently with my life totally out of control. And let's be honest, even though you paid cold, hard coin of the realm for this book, how many of you actually believe vampires are real now? Hmm? What's that? Oh, it's just fiction? Yeah, well, it's my life! I'm still coming to grips with the fact that vampires exist, along with shape shifters and faeries and God-only-knows-what else. I'm not about to be led by the hand back into line for another roller coaster ride, thank you very much. Whatever life had in store for me this time, I was going to keep as much control over things as I could.

It didn't take long to get a little control either. Jaeger figured out that I meant to camp there until he showed, so rather than listen to me call out to him again he came forward.

"I hate that you do that," he said to me.

"Then stop lurking around my property."

"I must do as my Magistrate orders."

"Does he order you not to talk to me?"

"Er, uh, no. He does not." That confused him.

"Good. Then from now on, simply let me know when you're going to be hanging around and we won't have any problems."

"I cannot do that."

"Why not?"

"Because…" He paused, searching for some kind of answer. Clearly he was not used to having anyone question what he did.

"Yeah, I thought so. Because it's not your SOP. Too bad. You want me to stop coming out here and calling to you, then you can check in with me and let me know you're around. Deal?"

He looked at me with a great deal of disgust. Amazing how quickly I'd gotten used to that. Nostrils flaring in a mini fit of indignation, he said "Fine, if that is the way it must be, but I do not like it."

"Oh, make no mistake, neither do I, but I'd rather know you are definitely out there than wonder what the hell is moving around in my bushes. Which reminds me, what are you doing here?"

"Ah!" he said with a smile. "That I cannot tell you. And yes, I have been ordered not to. So you can just forget about it."

I snorted at him. "Yeah right! Like that's gonna happen!" Standing up, I brushed the Pop Tart crumbs off of my legs and gathered up the empty wrapper and bottle of water. "Tell you what, why don't you and I just take a ride over to see Darius and he can tell me what this is all about." If I was going to take the bull by the horns, it might as well be the head bull.

Jaeger's jaw dropped. "You cannot just show up at the Magistrate's home and request to see him!"

"Why not? If he sent you to watch over me something important must be going on, so why wouldn't he see me?" The Hunter stammered a few more feeble excuses until I cut him off and said, "I'll go with you or without you, Jaeger. It's your choice."

Then I went and slipped on my Ked's, got my keys and purse, locked the door behind me and headed to my car. At the last moment, Jaeger zipped over to the passenger side and hopped in.

I didn't wait for him to buckle up, I just zoomed out of the driveway in reverse. What? He's already dead. Like an accident would hurt him! He took up way too much space in my new sports car. Close quarters with Jaeger. Oh yay.

Thankfully it wasn't too long a drive to get to the mansion. Well, frankly, anything longer than around the block was too long under the circumstances, but I could handle the twenty or so minutes, no matter how much the voices in my head were complaining.

"You seriously intend to go in there and expect to be seen?" Jaeger asked, clearly in utter disbelief as we neared Darius' home.

"Yes, I do. And I can't understand why it's so incredible. Give me a break! Like no one ever goes and asks to see him, ever? Pfft! Please!" Ok, so I didn't know for certain but it seemed pretty stupid to think no one ever went there requesting to see the Magistrate. I mean, come on, his position alone would dictate that sometimes vampires or other creatures would go seeking his guidance or advice or whatever, so this couldn't be a completely unheard of occurrence.

He just shook his head and went back to his silent, stoic stare out the front window. Vampires! I bet what he really cared about was whether or not Darius was going to hold him responsible for my coming.

Ok, ok. I can hear you, ya know? I know you're saying 'Hero, what are you doing?' Give me some credit. I'm not flying off the handle here. I had plenty of time to think while I ate my Pop Tarts. There is reason and logic behind this move. First, Mike said he heard Darius tell Jaeger to keep an eye on me. Which stands to reason because why else would Jaeger be haunting my front yard? Second, if Darius cares at all about what's going on at my house or with me, especially while Kin is away, that means something is wrong. After all, he sent in the big gun, Jaeger. Not like it was Mike that was looking after me. Ergo, something is going down, or on, or whatever, but it's something, and I either need protecting or watching. No matter how you look at it, we're talking muy importante and I'm not sitting at home in the dark waiting for something to happen.

So, off we go to see the Magistrate himself and find out just what the hell is going on. Sure, he probably isn't going to like it, but then again, neither do I.

I pulled into the parking area of the mansion and hopped out. Jaeger was already ahead of me before I even closed my door. "There's still time to change your mind."

"Jaeger, I know we don't know each other well, but honestly, what do you think the likelihood of that is?"

He sighed deeply. Actually, it was more like a low growl. Then he turned and strode briskly to the front door of the mansion. I had to trot to keep up with him, the jerk. Bet he got some dumb, male ego giggle out of it. Oooh, like it's so hard to walk faster than someone when you're nearly a foot taller than them. I stuck my tongue out at him. What? I was clearly behind his back at the time, don't panic.

There were several other, um, hmmm, I'm going to say vampires, waiting to see Darius when we got to the ante room. I didn't recognize any of them and had no reason to suspect they were anything other than vampires. The same imposing guard was standing at the door to Darius' office. I wondered if he ever got a break.

"Do you want to let them know I'm here, or should I?" I asked Jaeger with a little more bravado than I felt now that I was surrounded by almost a dozen vampires.

Jaeger grimaced and snorted. Very attractive. Not! "Wait," he said gruffly before stomping over to the guard. Ah, there was the Jaeger I'd come to know and ... Ok, well the Jaeger I'd come to know.

I took a seat in one of the gilt-trimmed chairs and tried not to pay attention to any of the vampires around me. I reached into my purse and turned the ringer off on my cell phone so I wouldn't draw any unwanted attention to myself. Who was I kidding? I was a human in a room full of vampires! Any attention was unwanted!

Ok, Hero, no time to get punchy. Think, think. How are you going to approach the situation with Darius? What if he's pissed off that you're here? I didn't think I could do that groveling, subservient thing that I'd seen some of the vamps do. In fact, I was pretty sure of it. Just witnessing it made the bile rise in my throat. I'd have to just try and stay unemotional and stick to the facts of the matter. Hey! Stop laughing. It could happen.

I'd just go in there and apologize for the interruption. Wait, hmm? Was that right? The interruption? No, then I'd be admitting that I'd interrupted him and I didn't want to own up to doing anything negative. Should I say for the unexpected visit? Yeah, that sounded better. An unexpected visit doesn't necessarily have to be a bad thing.

As I sat there inventing scenarios in my head, I couldn't help overhearing bits of a conversation between a group of vampires who had settled near me. Apparently, they didn't seem to think I was worth anything more than a late night snack and had no concern for speaking where I might hear them.

"But how could he have done it so easily? He was barely injured at all," said one vampire to his companions.

"He was injured enough for a healer to be called," stated a second vampire.

"A dislocated shoulder, I believe, and that was from a shifter, not from Nigel," added the third. Nigel! I admit, I wanted to turn and look at them so I could see them. I know, it was bad enough that I was listening to them; it would be bad on all kinds of levels to actually turn and look at them. I may be impulsive but I'm not stupid.

They were talking about Nigel and it sounded like maybe they were talking about Mike too. Mike had staked Nigel a few days ago during a battle at Hazel's house. Nigel was an old and ruthless vampire who belonged to a menagerie rather than a vampire clan. A menagerie was usually just for

47

shifters, but they welcomed any supernatural being that wanted to join them. Or at least that's how I understood it.

Mike was still just a fledgling. He'd only been a vampire for a matter of months. It had been a big deal that he'd defeated Nigel. But what the vampires didn't know, and I did, was that just prior to Mike taking Nigel down, Nigel had attacked Hazel and she had fended him off with a bloodstone. Faeries could wield bloodstone to temporarily weaken vampires. It was a secret that vampires had no idea of, and I had been trusted by Hazel and Lily not to tell.

Because of his severely weakened state, Mike was able to easily get the upper hand and stake Nigel with a branch from a tree in Hazel's yard. Needless to say, I wouldn't have told Mike even if I could have that it was because of faerie magic that he defeated Nigel. I believe it was the first time Mike had felt like he belonged to his new family. Plus it would have been mortifying for him.

Now other vampires were questioning it. It hadn't occurred to me that it was such an impossible thing for Mike to have done. I had figured they'd just think Mike had gotten lucky.

"It's little wonder he's come to question it. You know how he is when it comes to his children. And Nigel was one of his first."

He? He who? What the hell was this all about?

"But has Aton really come here? No one has actually seen him. It's just a rumor."

Ok, well that answered the 'who' part. If I was following this right, and I wasn't sure I was, Aton was Nigel's maker and there were rumors that he had come to the Boston area to check up on how an old and brutal vamp like Nigel could get staked by a newbie like Mike. So where the holy hell did I fit into all of this?

One of the other vampires began to respond but stopped abruptly. Oh damn! Did they figure out I was listening? I tried to look very interested in the laces of my Keds. Then I realized the whole room was still. Totally, completely still. I raised my head slowly and saw them all looking at me. Not a good feeling. Yeah, I'm sure you think you know, but keep in mind: Vampires 11, Humans 1. Uh huh.

Then I realized what was going on. To my ironic relief, I was getting what passed for the fish-eye from the apathetic guard at Darius' door, which means his eye that was facing me was fully opened, not the little half-slit it usually was.

I tried to smile, though why I don't really know, and I got up and walked over to the door. Mr. Personality let me right in and closed the door shut behind me. There was Darius sitting behind his big marble desk, just where I expected him to be.

This evening he was wearing a deep plum dress shirt with God knows what on the bottom because I couldn't see. Not like I cared. I approached the desk, hoping that was the right thing to do as he hadn't spoken yet. Stopping right in front of the desk, I nodded my head to him as I'd seen Kin do and said "Thank you for seeing me, Darius, I appreciate it."

Obediah, lurking in the shadows, winced at hearing me address his master by his Christian name. Sorry, pal, but I wasn't going to call him 'my liege' or anything like that.

Darius just raised an eyebrow. "Magistrate will do, thank you, Miss Fletcher. How may I help you?"

Lovely! Off to a great start. "I'm sorry, Magistrate. I'm not sure how your kind normally addresses each other, so if I should make any other slip ups, please know that they are not intentional. I come here with all due respect." He nodded. "I came to ask you why you have Jaeger hanging out at my place."

He pursed his lips and looked at me through narrowed eyes. I'm sure in his head he was thinking 'I don't have to tell you anything', but Darius was a diplomat, a consummate politician. Which is probably why he was the Magistrate.

"He is there because it pleases me to have him there."

I bit my lip. Literally. I'm sure you can guess the response that wanted to leap from my mouth on that one. "Forgive me, Magistrate, but I don't believe you." I said after a moment's consideration. I think if Obediah's heart was still beating it would have stopped.

"Is that so?" Darius replied darkly.

"I'm sorry, but yes, it is. I know Jaeger is very important to you and I can't believe that you would have him hanging around watching me just because you get a kick out of knowing what goes on at my house."

50

I held my breath then, waiting to see how my blunt honesty would be received. "You dare call the Magistrate a liar!" hissed Obediah at last, unable to keep quiet any longer.

Darius waved his hand and said "Thank you, Obediah. Your loyalty is steadfast as always." Oh, retch!

"Forgive me for upsetting you, Obediah. I mean no disrespect. I know important men sometimes lie because they believe it is in other's best interest to have the truth kept from them, not because they are dishonorable." I addressed myself to both vampires, hoping my point would be carried and score.

Obediah would not look at me. He stood silently staring into space. Darius, however, was another story. "So, you think I am hiding something from you for your own good, is that it, Miss Fletcher?"

"Yes, sir. Something along those lines anyway." Then I added, "I know you think I'm just a human, but I'm not stupid. I can see what's going on."

"And what is going on?"

"You have your number one guy stationed outside my home for one of two reasons. Either I need to be protected from someone or something, or you're protecting someone from me."

I give him credit, he tried not to scoff. Didn't make me any happier, but at least he tried not to. "It's my turn to ask forgiveness, Miss Fletcher, but who or what would need protecting from you?"

Every cell in my brain flooded with pithy comebacks. Some of them were really good too, but I couldn't use them. Not with Darius. Don't you hate that? What a waste of good sarcasm.

Instead, I took a deep breath and tried a new approach. "Magistrate," I began (and yes it hurt), "I am not here to make matters more difficult for you or cause any trouble. However, there is obviously something going on and you and I going round and round in circles isn't going to change that fact. Please, just tell me what's happening. Perhaps I may be of some help. You might be surprised. After all, I do know myself better than you do."

He gingerly placed his fingertips together and peered at me over the top of them, his dark brown eyes staring down his straight Roman nose. I couldn't help wondering if he could hear my heart beating. Everything else was so quiet and yet the sound of my heart was drumming loudly in my ears.

After what seemed like an eternity he said, "Sit down, Miss Fletcher." It wasn't a request. Nodding my assent, I reached behind and pulled up one of the French silk covered chairs and sat down. "Tell me what you think you know."

Not what I expected. "I don't know anything other than you've sent Jaeger to watch over me for some unexplained reason."

Darius considered me for a moment, then he pushed back from the desk and stood up. At least I got an answer to one of my questions. He was wearing black trousers with a fine white pinstripe. The Magistrate came around to the front of the desk and perched on the edge in front of me. "Jaeger informed me when you both arrived that you wish to be notified of his presence from now on. Is that correct?" I nodded. "You do not feel this might make you anxious?"

"Anxious? More anxious than constantly wondering if there is a vampire, or vampires or who knows what, lurking around outside my home? At least if I know that it's Jaeger out there I know it's one of the good guys and I'll feel safe."

It was Darius' turn to nod. "Mmm. Yes, a very human response I suppose. I had not considered it from that point of view."

"Yeah, well, I suppose that's to be expected after being dead for a few centuries." Oh holy crap! I said that out loud. I just hate when the inner monologue goes on the blink! "Oh! Dari... I mean, Magistrate, I'm..."

He just held his hand up to silence me. "Not to worry, Miss Fletcher. You may not have intended to say it, but it was an accurate statement nonetheless." I wasn't sure, but I think he very nearly smiled. Don't hold me to that though.

"Thank you," I muttered under my breath. I didn't worry about saying it softly. He was a vampire, I knew he could hear me.

"I know that Jaeger gave you no information as to his duties. However, it has been noted that the Fledgling Michael Avery visited you this evening. Did he tell you anything?"

I wasn't about to throw Mike under the bus. Hmm. Do you throw vampires under the bus or do you throw them under the hearse? Just seems more appropriate. Either way,

I wasn't going to do it. "Mike came to see me because he knows Kin is away and he wanted to check and see that I was ok and didn't need anything. Mike knows it's still a little difficult for me in my family home after everything that happened."

Darius stared at me for several moments. I'm not certain he believed me, but that was pretty much the truth. "Young Mr. Avery is a good friend."

"He is."

Darius shifted slightly so he was more directly in front of me. "Are you aware of the heroic service he did you during the battle last week?"

Whoa oh! Tread carefully, Hero! "I had heard something about it. Mike is modest. He didn't want to discuss such things."

This received a doubting look in reply. I know, you're shocked. "So you are aware that he staked Nigel."

I nodded. We sat in very uncomfortable silence for a few moments and then Darius rose again. He walked behind me, which was not a good feeling. I wanted to swivel around and keep my eye on him, but that would hardly have been appropriate. "Are you also aware that Nigel was seven hundred years old?"

Keep calm, keep calm. "No, how would I know a thing like that. All I knew about him was that he was some freak who showed up on my front lawn and turned out to be a henchman for the psycho cat-woman that was ruining my life.

54

And when she decided to try and take me out he helped her and got taken down. End of story." Ok, forget calm. I just hoped my rambling made sense!

"Unn huh. I see. Then you had no reason to find it strange that a recently born vampire such as Mr. Avery could defeat him?"

"I'm sorry, but no. Something like that wouldn't occur to me. You have to remember, I've only recently discovered you guys are even real. Not that I mean any disrespect, but you do a good job of pretending not to exist."

He rested his hands on the back of my chair and continued, (I think he chose to ignore my comment about finding out vampires were real, and frankly, I was glad, but oh so not happy about where he was standing.) "You were inside Miss Greenleaf's house during the whole battle, is that correct?" I nodded. "Were you able to see anything going on outside; from a window, perhaps?"

"No, I stayed away from the one window in the room. I didn't want Leontine to know where I was. By the time Angel came in to help me, I think it was all pretty much over."

What was going on here? The tables had been turned. I was being interrogated. Had Darius heard the gossip too? Was Aton or whatever the hell his name was really here looking into Nigel's death? And really, what was up with that? They're vampires. They were in a battle. Some of them were going to die. My mind was racing. What to do? Obviously I wasn't about to say anything about what I knew of the situation. I couldn't for multiple reasons, which you already know. And if you don't, pay more attention!

But, do I play completely dumb and hope Darius lets me in on what's going on or do I tip my hand just a little? He had left his position behind me, which I was enormously glad of, and was headed back to his seat behind his grand marble desk. "Well, Miss Fletcher, thank you for your visit and I will be sure to instruct Jaeger to inform you when he is on your property."

Oh, Darius! You don't know me at all yet, buddy. Yes, I was afraid of you, very afraid, but Mrs. Fletcher didn't raise any fools and she sure as hell didn't raise any doormats. "When he's on my property? I see. So you tell him to keep on the outer edge of my property and he doesn't have to tell me anything. I'm sorry, that's not good enough."

As you can imagine, this didn't make Darius too happy, as he began to work up to his 'Don't mess with me, human, I'm the Magistrate' face and whole pose, I decided to go ahead and show my cards. I figured it was my only chance at getting a clue as to what was going on.

"And what are all these questions about Mike and the battle at Hazel's? Surely, that can't have anything to do with Jaeger stalking me. You said it was all set, that you'd reached an agreement with Ilderim. So..."

I let it trail off just for a moment, waiting to see if he'd bite or if I'd have to give him some more line. Nothing. Damn! "Wait," I continued, pretending it had only just now occurred to me, "in the other room, while I was waiting," I said while pointing unnecessarily to the room behind me. "I heard some men, uh vampires, talking about how some defeated vampire's maker had come to investigate his death. Is that what this is about? Is Nigel's maker looking for revenge? Is that why I need to be protected?"

Even as I said it I felt sick to my stomach. I'd been thinking that in the back of my head since I eavesdropped on those vampires, but saying out loud, that made it real.

Obediah was once again clearly agitated. I think he would have loved to have thrown me out via the roof. I just got the same old cold stare from Darius. I had to resist the urge to wave my hand in front of his face and say 'Hello? Anybody home?' Yes, I am capable of resisting sometimes.

After what seemed like ages Darius finally spoke. "There have been some questions raised and until they are concluded it would be better if you allowed Jaeger to be near you."

"And by better, you mean safer."

"Yes, Miss Fletcher. Safer."

"But why? I didn't do anything?" I was sick of the unfair treatment of humans buy supernatural creatures.

"Because you were the reason there was a battle. You are the catalyst that caused Nigel's death."

Chapter 5

Well! Isn't that just great! And the hits just keep on coming! Thus the old adage about getting what you wish for.

As I drove back home I imagined I saw shapes in every shadow, eyes staring back in every reflective surface. I was a mess by the time I reached Georgia Road. I tried to tell myself it was better the devil you know than the devil you don't, except, I didn't know this Aton character. I suppose at least I knew what was going on and why Jaeger was hanging around. Who knows what my over-active imagination might have thought up?

I quickly fled from the car into my home, slamming the door and resetting the alarm. Naturally, I knew Jaeger would be right behind me, but I also knew vampires were quick and it would only take a second or two for Aton or some other vampire to get me if Jaeger were delayed even a moment.

No sooner had I set the alarm than there was a sharp knock on the door. Great! Jaeger reporting for duty. "Thanks, Jaeger. I know you don't...."

It wasn't Jaeger. There was a tall, lean, dark-skinned man on my doorstep. He was bald and his eyes were jet black. The corner of his mouth raised slightly and he said "I am not Jaeger." His voice reminded me of Yul Bryner.

The hairs on my arms stood on end and instinctively, I took a step back. "You may not come into my home," I said. He smiled fully now. It was a cold, cruel smile.

"That is fine."

"You are Aton, aren't you?"

"Ah, you have heard of me?"

"Just your name," I replied. "What do you want here?"

"The truth, Miss Fletcher. I want the truth."

"You already know it."

"No, I do not believe I do." He titled his head downward ever so slightly, creating a hood over those dark, stony eyes.

God help me, I felt compelled to speak. "There was a battle. Nigel had been fighting many people. Mike caught him unexpectedly and got lucky. End of story. It was a fluke."

"A fluke? Flukes such as that do not happen to vampires, Miss Fletcher."

"Don't they? I don't see why not. They happen to every other living creature on this planet. Why are vampires exempt?"

His head snapped around swiftly. "I regret I must end our discussion. We will meet again." And with that, he was gone.

Before I had a chance to draw another breath Jaeger had taken his place on the doorstep. "Are you all right?"

"Yes, he just spoke to me." Even though that was the case I still couldn't help shaking. Something told me that he was the most heartless, vicious vampire I'd met yet. I couldn't shake the feeling of looking into the eyes of a snake.

"What did he say?" I relayed the conversation to Jaeger, who would no doubt retell it to Darius. "How did you know it was him?" asked Jaeger.

I shook my head. "I don't know. Something in the way he looked at me. Like," I paused to swallow," like he expected me to know him."

"I will be here to keep watch the rest of the night. Do not worry."

"Thank you, Jaeger," I said, and I truly meant it. I went in and shut the door and then I recalled something important.

"Jaeger! Wait!" I called out. "Aton, he's probably in touch with members of Ilderim's menagerie, isn't he?" Jaeger nodded. I felt ill. Swallowing hard I said "Jaeger, I give you permission to enter my home." His eyes opened wide. "No sense in taking any chances this time," I said. Again he nodded, his hardened face revealing he got my full meaning, and then he disappeared into the darkness.

If Aton should enlist the aid of any shifters from the menagerie, they don't need permission to enter my home. If one should get in and Jaeger didn't have an invitation into my home, he was useless to me.

I checked the alarm one more time and headed for the kitchen. Grabbing an iced tea from the fridge and some Ring

Dings from the cabinet, I then trudged upstairs to my bedroom. Oh, Ring Dings, Ring Dings! What happened to the days when you could solve most of my problems?

Yes, I admit, I have a chocolate addiction. I'm not ashamed. There are a great many worse things in this world a person could have issues with. Let him among you without such a sin throw the first emotional crutch.

Things didn't look much better in the light of day. What was this world coming to? Chocolate was letting me down. Wasn't that a sign of the Apocalypse? Please let this just be a temporary bad phase or else there just might not be any reason to go on living!

What in the world was I going to do about the whole Mike/Nigel/Aton thing? Aton. What kind of name was that anyway? I kept wanting to say Anton. Show of hands, how many of you keep wanting to read it that way? Uh huh, yeah, I thought so. You're not alone.

Kin was in some other country. I couldn't call him and worry him. Well, not again. I couldn't call Mike and worry him. That would just be cruel. But I had to talk to someone. Well, that left just one person. No, no. Not Jaeger. We might have called a truce of sorts but he wasn't exactly my best pal.

So, I called the only other person I could. Hazel. I was a bit nervous, especially since our last meeting didn't go too well but I couldn't think of anyone else.

"Hi, Hazel," I said when she answered. "Would it be ok if I came over?" I wasn't going to ask her to put herself out and come to me.

She sounded her usual happy self and said she'd love to see me. This was a great relief. I pulled myself together and headed out to my car. I caught a glimpse of black boots poking out of the bushes along the side of my driveway. Very subtle. Under my breath I sing-songed "Going to Hazel's" before breaking into a chipper, random scat.

Hopefully, Jaeger heard me, and no one else did. I took the long way around and stopped at a bakery along the way to pick up some cinnamon rolls. I figured if anyone else was following me, this would help give Jaeger a chance to see them. But really, what the hell did I know about vampire surveillance?

Once at Hazel's I resisted the urge to look around and see if my body guard was there. Hazel greeted me at the door and ushered me right in.

"It's good to see you," she said cheerfully. "Oh! What have you brought?" she asked, excited to see the bakery box.

This was the Hazel I was used to. It was good to see her back to her usual self. We sat and had tea and cinnamon rolls and chatted about all sorts of nonsense. It was great!

After about an hour I asked, "Hazel, do you know who Aton is?"

She stopped abruptly and blanched. "Yes. But how do you?"

"He came to my house last night." I replied simply.

Hazel closed her eyes and muttered something under her breath. "Are you ok?"

"Of course I am. Do you think I'd have been sitting here with you like this if I wasn't?"

Nodding, she asked "What did he say to you?"

"He's asking about Nigel and Mike. He finds it strange that Mike was able to defeat him."

Hazel did not miss the importance of my words. Nor did she misunderstand my tone. She knew that I was aware of the secret I possessed and that I was keeping it for her and Lily.

"Thank you, Hero, for not telling. I'm sure that was difficult." She was deflated now. All the normal exuberance that characterized Hazel whisked away.

"No, not difficult at all. I was a little worried that Darius might not believe that I didn't know anything, but it wasn't hard to keep a secret for my friends."

"Darius! Oh my! You've spoken to Darius about this?" Poor Hazel was clearly agitated.

"Yes, I wanted to know why he had Jaeger watching me."

This stopped her again. "Hold on. You went to Darius and asked him why he had Jaeger watching you?"

"Yes, I did. What's so strange about that? Why is it so incredible that people might actually just go and ask Darius direct questions?"

"Because they rarely do. He's a vampire magistrate, Hero. Normally, if he wants you to know something, you know it, and if he doesn't…" She let her sentence trail off.

"Well, I asked him. It was a bit uncomfortable and he asked more questions than he answered, but all in all it was fine." Ok, maybe 'fine' wasn't exactly accurate, but he didn't kill me or even yell at me. Though since the meeting I'd had enough time to realize that the only reason it had gone as well as it had was that he had wanted to get information from me. It served his purposes for me to be there.

She shook her head at me. "You amaze me sometimes, Hero."

I just shrugged. "So, this Aton guy. What's going on with him? Does he suspect anything about the faeries?"

"Not that we've heard. There are so many rumors, but some are speculating that Mike used something to give himself an edge over Nigel."

"Well, I can't imagine what one vampire would use over another, but what if he did? It was a battle. I thought a vampire battle was 'everything goes'?"

Hazel grimaced. "Mmmm. It sort of is. There are a few things that are considered dishonorable. Not that they aren't used from time to time, but… You know how vampires are when it comes to their honor."

I did. It was stupid. I've got nothing against honor, or dignity or any of those other qualities, but a lot of vamps seemed to take it to an almost psychotic level. "What kinds of things?"

She thought for a minute. "Like a stun gun or a regular gun. They won't kill or even seriously harm another vamp, but they will slow him down considerably for several seconds, and all you need are a few seconds. Spells and magic obtained from other sources. Basically, anything that isn't natural to you as a vampire or just as handy a weapon in your environment for your opponent. Like, if you use some foreign object for a weapon, it should be something found where you are fighting that your opponent has or had equal access to."

"So, no bringing your own weapons. Gotcha. Then that means they must think Mike used some kind of magic? If he'd had a gun or Taser, there'd have been evidence of it." Hazel looked at me knowingly. "So, what the holy heck does that have to do with me? I'm a human! He sure didn't get any magic or spells from me."

We sat quietly for a few minutes contemplating the whole scenario. "I asked Darius why I needed to be protected. He said it was because I was the catalyst for the whole battle. Does that mean if Aton can't find someone to blame for Nigel's death, he'll blame me?"

"Oh!" cried Hazel. "No, that can't be!" But even as she said it, I could see she was afraid for me.

I lay down and curled up in a ball on Hazel's sofa. "Is it afternoon yet?" I asked.

"Why?"

"I think I need one of your cocktails. Or two, or maybe three."

Hazel and I shared several cocktails. Well, I had several cocktails. Hazel had one that she nursed for hours. Faeries can't hold their liquor. I was in a really sucky position. I had a big secret to keep. Not only was the secret being kept so Mike didn't lose face in front of all the other vampires and lose confidence in himself, but I was keeping a very serious secret for all of faeriedom. Hmmm. That doesn't come up in spellcheck. If faeriedom is not a word yet, I want credit when Webster's adds it.

But, if I hung on to this very important, top secret, secret, I might bear the brunt of Aton's fury at losing Nigel to a fledgling vampire. And God only knows what that might entail. Even death.

I think you'll all agree, not an enviable position to be in. Having wallowed all I dared in Hazel's presence, after all, I didn't want to make her feel bad that she'd confided in me, I decided it was time to head home. I could always continue my wallowing there. I'd had plenty of practice.

We said our good-byes and I went out to my Sebring convertible. I had put the top up earlier to help hide my identity on the way over. Now, I stood at the driver's door, fumbling for my keys in my over-crowded purse.

Because of the drinks, my reactions were slowed. I heard something. A slight rustle. But it took too long to register. By the time I turned my head to look for the source, he was upon me. In a flash I was scooped up over someone's broad shoulder and hurried away from my car and Hazel's driveway more quickly than I was able to comprehend. The superfast movement knocked the wind out of me.

By the time my befuddled mind caught up with what was going on and I was able to start protesting, my captor put me down inside the cargo area of a small panel truck. I tried to scream, to climb to my feet, but two strong arms shoved me backwards, knocking me onto the hard floor and all the air came rushing out of my stomach a second time. The doors slammed shut and I heard the locks clicking into place.

Using the wall of the truck to brace myself, I stood and started calling for help, banging on the wall with my fists. "No one can hear you, Miss Fletcher," said a deep voice with a foreign accent.

I whipped around and flattened my back against the wall. Aton stepped towards me from the dark recesses of the truck interior. A razor thin sliver of light that squeezed in from the door allowed us to see each other's outlines and the vague contours of our faces, but not much else. "Leave me alone!" I cried feebly. "I don't know anything!"

Aton came close to me, staring into my blue eyes with his cold black ones. "Perhaps and perhaps not. Time will tell. But those who do know may be willing to tell in order to secure your safety, would they not, Miss Fletcher?"

Oh holy crap! "I, I don't know. I told you, it was just a fluke. There isn't anything to tell. How is anyone supposed to tell you anything when there's nothing?" I was in full panic now and the buzz from the alcohol was wearing off quickly.

He smiled that cold, cruel smile again. Even in the dark, I somehow felt it more than saw it. "We both know there was no fluke, Miss Fletcher. No, no. You see, I trained Nigel. I worked with him for hundreds of years. He was the best. Even had there been, as you say, a 'fluke', there would have been some sign that Nigel and Mr. Avery had fought one another. There is no such evidence. It is almost as if Nigel allowed himself to be staked, and naturally, that was not the case."

"I really don't know. I was inside the house. I didn't see any of it. I've never seen a vampire battle. I don't know how things normally go. Maybe it's because I'm a human, but it seems very possible to me that Mike could have had the tree branch or whatever it was he had, Nigel had been fighting someone else, turned around, not knowing Mike was behind him and in that one second of surprise at seeing Mike, Mike got his chance and staked him. Sure, it's one shot in a million, but I still think it's a reasonable explanation." I wasn't even sure of what I was saying, I was so freaking afraid I just kept babbling because if I was talking at least I was alive.

"Indeed," he said cryptically. "You are right, from the human perspective that probably does sound like a remote possibility. From the vampire perspective, it sounds like a faerie tale."

I had to resist the urge to laugh. The irony was obviously lost on him. The truck took a corner and I nearly fell to the floor, sliding along the wall. Aton reached out and stood me back up. I would have rather fallen.

"So what happens now? Where are you taking me?"

"I am taking you someplace where we will wait for one of your friends to tell us what we wish to know."

We? Was this the royal We or were there others involved? Duh, Hero! Obviously there were others. The truck wasn't driving itself. But I still wondered just how many others made up this 'we'.

"And what if they don't tell you what you want to know? Of what if you realize what they are already telling you is the actual truth?"

"Well then, Miss Fletcher. I guess I will have to hold you responsible for the death of my child."

"What? No way! How is it my fault? If it was anyone's fault, it was Leontine's. She got him involved. She's the one that disobeyed the order. I would have been more than happy to have Nigel just stay as far away from me as possible."

"Leontine is dead," he said without a trace of emotion.

"So, this isn't really about finding out who is responsible. This is just about getting revenge and taking a life for a life," I said after thinking about it for a minute.

"Mmmm. Yes, I suppose you could say that. No matter how you look at it, Nigel should not have died and now someone must pay the price."

"And you don't really care who that is, do you?" I asked, so hoping that I was wrong.

He shrugged. "No, actually. If there is not clearly someone to blame, then no, Miss Fletcher, I do not really care who pays."

Chapter 6

I'd like to revisit that issue with God screwing with me. At the moment, I'm having difficulty believing in God at all, but if there is no God, there is no Heaven. If there is no Heaven, then I'll never see my mom again. So, therefore, there must be a Heaven and a God. We all rationalize to get through life and you have just experienced one of mine.

Oh, God! Really, what is going on up there? I've tried to be a good person. Yeah, ok, I killed Leontine, but it was self-defense. I wouldn't have done it if there was any other way out. Cut me some slack! The past few weeks have been really rough. I know you're not supposed to give us more than we can handle but I think perhaps you might be over estimating me. Have you met my mom up there? Is she talking me up? Mothers have a tendency to brag, you know. Especially about single daughters in their thirties. Take anything she says with a grain of salt.

Of course, this conversation was all held in my head. No, not because I'm a mental case, but because I didn't want the vampires in the next room to hear me talking to God. I wasn't ashamed or anything, I just think things like that should be private.

As I sat in the bare little room with a shoddy looking twin bed, a metal folding chair and a card table, I couldn't help but recall Kin's story of how he was made a vampire. I hadn't had a good look at the other vampires as I was hurried into the bedroom from the panel truck, but none of them looked like a 'Clive' to me.

I hadn't any idea where I was. I couldn't even tell if I was in a house or an apartment or who knows where. There were no windows in the room, which made me wonder if it were an office building of some kind. I could hear nothing except the occasional scrap of muffled conversation from my captives on the other side of the door.

They'd shoved me in here without a word. Very unceremonious of them. No one had come to check on me, ask me questions or offer me so much as a glass of water. I guess I shouldn't expect them to remember I'm not a vampire and need to eat and drink.

I had no idea of how much time had passed, nor did I know how long I had been shut inside the truck with Aton. My tipsy condition had made the beginning of that trip a bit hazy. It might have been five minutes, it might have been fifteen, before I began to get my wits about me. In the Greater Boston area, depending on where you're going and how you're getting there, a difference of ten minutes can be enormous. I'd been taken from Hazel's place in Milton. The highways go everywhere from there. I could be in Boston or North, West or South; a myriad of destinations easily accessible from that starting point.

There was no way for me to pass the time in the tiny room. I could sit here staring at the four walls or I could crawl into bed and take a nap. I voted for the first option. Falling asleep was not going to happen.

What was happening out there? Had calls been made or messengers dispatched? Was Hazel ok? Did Darius know what had taken place? Where was Jaeger? How had they gotten past him? And what about Kin? Would Darius tell him? Probably not. He wouldn't want to risk Kin leaving before the job was done again.

The real question: Would any of them rescue me? Hazel and Lily couldn't let the secret of the bloodstone be known. Darius certainly wouldn't sacrifice any of his people for me. If it came down to a life for Nigel's, Darius would see me dead before a vampire. Correction. Would see me dead before he'd see a vampire dead again.

Aha! There was something to do to pass the time after all. Panic! Yup, panic finally set in. Oh crap! I was going to die. I survived the stupid cat-bitch just to be killed anyway.

I ran my hands through my long dark hair and stood to pace the short open distance in the little room. Desperately I tried to convince myself that this was not happening, that somehow Kin and his friends would save me. Ugh, God! Damsel in distress crap, I hate that! I don't want people to have to save me. Well, who does really? I want to be able to take care of myself.

The panic was doing a great job of making me nuts because I could clearly hear my father lecturing me on the dangers of making poor choices when it comes to companions. Gee, thanks Dad, that's coming in real handy right about now. Get out of my head!

The voices in my head were all clamoring to be heard. Some just wanted to whine and complain. Some were afraid. One wise ass wanted to say 'I told you so'. Others wanted to devise grandiose schemes of escape. Don't pretend like you don't all have voices in your heads. We might joke about them and make psycho jokes about the Son of Sam etc, but that's a totally different type of 'Voice'. You know all your thoughts go bouncing around in your head and you don't just think them, you 'hear' them. So don't judge.

I tried pressing my ear against the door to see if I could hear what was going on in the other room. No good. I could hear that there were multiple voices but I couldn't make out what they were saying. Now and then I thought I recognized my name or Darius' name, but I wasn't sure. It was infuriating. I contemplated jumping up and down on the bed like a child having a temper tantrum. At least it would have been something to do.

Perhaps I'd read too many Nancy Drew books as a kid, but I decided to run my hands along the wall and look for secret devices. Why? I have no freaking idea. I was getting cabin fever; I was panicking, afraid for my life. It was something to do. Something to focus on.

Carefully, I took one step over from the door and ran my hands slowly in a back and forth pattern across the wall, mentally making note of where I stopped vertically so I could match the next section to it.

I proceeded in this fashion for several minutes, going all the way down to the base board and as high as my short frame would allow. There was nothing.

I scrutinized the hardwood floor that had seen better days and saw nothing of interest there either. So, I plunked myself back down in the butt-numbing folding chair and tried to give in to waiting.

"Miss Fletcher."

I awoke with a start. I had fallen asleep in the chair, my head resting on the card table. Aton had come into the room while I was sleeping and had brought a chair with him. He was now seated across from me.

"I'm sorry to have woken you."

"Yeah, I'm sure you're all broken up about it," I said as I rubbed my eyes and straightened up. "What time is it?"

"That's not important."

"Maybe not to you. I'm not immortal. Time still matters to me." You could say I'd woken up on the wrong side of the card table, but, considering what was on the other side of the card table....

He was unmoved. "I was wondering if now that you have had time to think about your situation you might have something more to tell me."

"Huh?" I said, jerking back and giving my best 'Whatchyou talking 'bout, Willis' face. "More to tell you? Like how pissed I am that you've locked me in here like this? Nothing to do, no one to talk to, nothing to eat or drink, no bathroom."

Aton raised his hand. "You know what I mean, Miss Fletcher."

"No, clearly I don't. Do you mean that after subjecting me to this I'm supposed to suddenly have some epiphany or that you want me to have crafted some humongous lie that will make you feel better about Nigel dying?"

"Don't try my patience!" he scolded.

"Look, I've told you all that I know. I was inside, unable to see what was going on. Ask any of the menagerie that were there. At no point during the battle was I outside. I have no idea what went down between those two or what might have taken place just before or anything else that was going on at the same time, or frankly anything at all. There was a battle. Leontine managed to get inside the room where I was hiding. She attacked me, I defended myself, Angel came and helped me. By the time I managed to make it outside it was all over and just about everybody was gone. That's it. There ain't no more."

Aton was grinding his teeth. "I believe you know more than you are letting on."

"What in the world makes you think that?"

"Because I know you went to visit Mr. Avery after the battle. That you spent the entire next day with him and that he came to visit you last night."

Steady, Hero. Keep cool, girl. I sighed in exasperation. "Oh please!" I began. "First off, I met Mike the same time I met Angel and Hazel when Kin asked them to help clean up the mess Leontine had made of my house. After the battle, I met Lily who brought me back to see Darius. Darius said I had to stay at the mansion. Since I had just had to fight for my life, I decided I'd stay. I asked Lily to take me to see Hazel. I wanted to see her and thank her for all her help. She had risked her life for me. When we left Hazel's room, Angel was in the hall and told us Mike would really like to see us, see us both, so we went to see him. The next day, I had no idea what I was supposed to do while I waited at the mansion for Kin. Mike found me and offered to keep me company. We played pool all day. That was all. Then yesterday, he had heard Kin was away and wanted to come and check on me. He knows I'm still adjusting to all the changes at my house since Leontine wrecked it and was just being nice. That's all there is to it." I gave him a look that clearly indicated he was crazy if he thought there was something else too it.

"That's how you want to play it?"

"I'm not playing anything. That's how it *is*."

Aton stood and went to the door. He inserted a key in the lock and opened it up. "Gentlemen, it appears I will be needing your assistance," he said.

Two vampires entered the room. One had short, close cropped dark hair. He looked like a body builder, broad and muscular. The other had medium length blonde hair and was athletically built. Clearly strong and muscular, but not as developed as his counterpart.

My heart was hammering in my chest so hard I thought it would explode. "Who are they?" I asked, not really caring what their names were but frantic to keep them talking rather than doing.

That same cold, cruel smile crept across Aton's lips. "This is Alex," he said nodding toward the blonde, "and this is Bradley," he said indicating the brunette. I'm sure under other circumstances I would've found a vampire named Bradley amusing.

"Say 'hello' to Miss Fletcher gentlemen."

"Hello," they said flatly, in unison. The pair looked at me without emotion as though they were robots, automatons. Stepford Vampires.

"I can see that you are very nervous, Miss Fletcher. Good. You should be. I will give you one last chance to tell me what you know."

I thought I would vomit but that would have required too much effort. I couldn't muster that much exertion at that point. "I, I've t-told you. I d-don't know any-anything else. P-please."

Before I could utter another syllable, they were upon me; Alex on my left and Bradley on my right. Each held one arm behind my back and their other hands were placed firmly on my thighs. All I could move was my head. That is, until they both bent their own heads into the crook of my neck and bit.

The pain was excruciating. I wanted to scream but no sound would come out. I couldn't move, and there across from me stood Aton smiling. Not that cold smile but a smile of joy. He was loving every second of this. Those terrible snake eyes were gleaming with excitement.

Was this it? Were they going to drain me and just use me as the scapegoat for Nigel's death? Or were they going to turn me into one of them to take Nigel's place?

Whether it was the pain, the shock, the loss of blood or all three I don't know, but mercifully, I lost consciousness.

When I awoke it took me several minutes to remember where I was and what had happened. The fog of sleep was so heavy and was in no hurry to dissipate. As I tossed and turned my head in frustration at my inability to fully wake and recall where I was, the scent of bleach, strong and acrid, filled my nostrils and acted as a stimulant, helping to clear the cobwebs. But as the fragments of my memory slid back into place I found myself wishing they were again shattered.

I wanted to raise my hands to my neck and feel where Alex and Bradley had fed off of me but I was too afraid. My arms remained stiffly by my side. Silent tears ran down the sides of my face, dripping onto the pillow and running into my ears. I was too afraid to move, too afraid to make a sound, so I just lay there and cried noiselessly.

The windowless room made it impossible to have any idea how much time had passed. I didn't know if it was the same day or the next day or even the day after that. Again I was reminded of the story of Kin's change from human to vampire and it terrified me.

I didn't want to become a vampire, but I didn't want to die either. What a choice! Hell A or Hell B! What were they planning? And it wouldn't be horrible enough to be made vampire, but I'd be a thing of Aton's. I'd belong to him for eternity. One more reason to vote for death.

I started to laugh to myself in that hysterical way people do when they're losing their minds. All I could think of was those sappy vampire romance stories where the girl *wants* to become a vampire so she and her lover can be together forever. Maybe it's because Kin and I haven't been together long, or maybe I'm just a lot more sane than I felt, but I can't imagine anyone wanting to have this done to them.

If they turn me I will have to leave my whole life behind. My childhood home that is so precious to me. All of my friends who are more of a family to me than the family I have remaining. Who would look after my mom's grave site and make sure it's watered and the flowers are nice? What about my business that I've worked so hard to build? And I'd have to keep starting over again and again and again because I wouldn't age. Plus, let's not forget the added bonus of a strict diet of blood! Ugh! And no chocolate! That wasn't a joke, I was completely serious about that.

Never having anything even remotely resembling a normal life again and having to do it over and over and over for centuries while I slowly lose my humanity. Yeah, sure! Sign me up for that! I don't think so.

Well, that tramped the laughter out of me; hysterical and otherwise.

I have no idea if I'm going to live through this, and if I do, I have no idea whether I'll ever get married and have children, but I just want to say for the record, right here, right now, if I ever have a teenage daughter who thinks it would be romantic to be made a vampire so she and her sparkly boyfriend can be together forever I will beat the crap out of her. I don't believe it hitting your kids, but given my present state of mind that seems the only reasonable reaction. Who knows, I could change my mind. Maybe.

Oh, and if you're reading this and you're a fan of those stories, I've read them, I've seen the movies and I am not knocking them. Great entertainment, but there's a big difference between being entertained and being delusional. I'm just saying.

After lying there for what seemed like ages I gave in and moved my right arm to scratch and itch. To my relief, nothing hurt. I tested my left arm. That seemed ok too. Slowly I raised myself into a sitting position. My shoulders were slightly stiff as was my neck, but I wasn't going to let myself think about that.

Gingerly, I swung my legs over the side of the bed and stood up. I felt a bit shaky for a moment but it passed quickly. After making a couple of rounds about the tiny room I sat in the folding chair and began contemplating my fate all over again.

I felt like a rag doll. My limbs were limp and I couldn't hold my head up. Wearily, I lay my head upon my arm. My mouth was so dry. I hadn't eaten or drank since I had been at Hazel's. I wasn't hungry. Believe it or not, food held no appeal for me, but I would have loved a Diet Sprite.

Ugh! Just thinking about it made me thirstier. I thought of all the old movies I'd seen, and all the spoofs of old movies I'd seen where the character crawls on their hands and knees through the desert gasping for water. In spite if myself, I managed a weak chuckle as I thought of *Spaceballs* and Mel Brooks having his princess gasping for room service. At least I still had my sense of humor. That was something. Ok, maybe not, but I would take what I could get.

I rolled my eyes in the direction of the door, calculating the odds of it being unlocked. Slim to none. Closer to none. Not worth the effort of standing up and going over there and twisting the knob. So I decided to calculate some more odds. What was more likely to happen? Would someone come in the room to check on me, and maybe let me have a drink or use the bathroom if I stared at the door and wished for it to happen, or if I stared at the door and wished for it not to happen? Not very scientific, I know, but I wasn't up to my usual level of mental stimuli.

After a few minutes I found that not only did I not care anymore, but I was confusing myself. Man! How much blood had they taken? I was so weak and tired. Part of me wanted to crawl back over to the bed but it seemed so far away. Like four or five whole giant steps. Maybe three steps and a really good flop. No, I don't think I could manage a flop. I'd probably end up on the floor.

Not that they'd care if I did! I thought angrily and I returned my attention, such as it was, to the bedroom door. I narrowed my eyes and shot what I hoped were daggers at the imaginary images of Aton, Alex and Bradley on the other side of the door. In actuality, they were probably more like toothpicks. The thin dull ones with the rounded ends that snap easily.

That small, ineffectual and completely unknown-outside-of-my-head act of defiance wiped out what miniscule bit of energy I had managed to recoup. In a matter of seconds, I was asleep at the table again.

Chapter 7

"Miss Fletcher?"

Oh crap! Not again. This time I didn't jump. "This is becoming a habit," I replied as I sat up.

"You seem to have developed some very nasty habits. I wish you would break yourself of them."

"Like telling the truth?"

He started to glower at me but I kept talking. "Look, I appreciate the whole terror tactics, I really do. But if you're going to keep me here is there any chance I can use the bathroom and maybe get something to eat or drink? 'Cause otherwise you might as well just kill me now."

I wish I could describe his expression. What is it with vampires? Are they really so used to never having anyone question them or have a different agenda? That was getting old so quick. I also think that perhaps I was just a bit delirious. Dehydration will do that to you.

"You are hardly in the position to make demands, Miss Fletcher."

"Demands? Nah, more like helpful suggestions. I have to pee, I'm thirsty as all hell and if you think you're going to get anywhere with any human in a state like this you're just setting yourself up for disappointment." I had a hard time getting that last part out. My tongue was starting to feel too big for my mouth.

"Oh, you will talk! Alex! Bradley!"

The vampire pair appeared and flanked me in an instant. "Hey, the gang's all here!" I muttered as I put my head down on the table again. Inside I was scared as hell, but I also knew there was nothing I could do. I wouldn't let Aton have the satisfaction of letting him see me scared. I gave in to the fatigue and the fear and let myself go limp. They could have me, but I wasn't going to make it easy.

Each of the sidekicks grabbed a side as they had before. This time however, my head lolled around and I was slumped down instead of rigid. The dynamic duo did their best to hoist me up and get me to be afraid. I wasn't going to play.

"Imbeciles!" Aton cried after a few more moments of buffoonery. He swept them away with one arm and grabbed my throat with his other hand, lifting me out of the chair.

"Have I got your attention now, Miss Fletcher?" he asked as he held me up, my feet dangling, my hands clawing at his. He held me too tightly for me to speak. I communicated what I hoped was acquiescence with my eyes. It must have been the right expression because he dropped me back onto the hard metal chair.

"Uph!" I huffed as I landed, my hands now grasping where only a few minutes ago they had wanted desperately to avoid. I could feel the tender skin where Aton had squeezed

84

my neck but I could also feel the marks where Alex and Bradley had drunk from me. I felt ill.

I looked down at my lap wondering if the bathroom issue had resolved itself while Aton had choked me. I was dry. Thank goodness for small favors.

"Are you ready to speak to me now?" asked Aton in a haughty, superior tone.

"Drink, please," I croaked feebly, still grasping my neck.

Aton eyed me suspiciously for a moment and then nodded to Bradley. In a flash of vampire super speed, Bradley zoomed out of the room and returned with a glass of water. It was tepid and clearly tap water but I didn't care. It was wet. That was all that mattered at the moment. I drank it down greedily, coughing a little at first as it cooled my injured throat.

Patiently, Aton waited for me to finish my drink and catch my breath before he started questioning me. I couldn't decide if this was because he enjoyed prolonging the process or because he thought he was lulling me into some false sense of… I don't know. Security sure as hell wasn't going to happen.

"Well?" I said at last.

"Well, are you ready to speak to me?" I nodded. "Very good. Now tell me the truth."

Tears welled up in my eyes. "I have been, I swear. Do you think if I knew anything else that I'd put myself through this? If I knew anything, anything at all, no matter how small or stupid of whatever, I would tell you in the hopes that you would let me out of here, but I don't!" I began to cry in earnest. "I just want to get out of here and forget I even met real vampires! If I knew something I'd tell you! I just want to go home! I just want to go home!" I bent my head to the table again and sobbed. I had no idea how this would go over. I didn't think vampires would react well to such overblown female emotions, but I also thought it was my best bet for convincing him I was telling the truth.

Aton pounded his fist on the table. "Do you think I'm a fool?!"

"No!" I cried, raising my head.

"Then why do you persist in this charade! Tell me what I want to know!"

"I wish I could! I do! I can't think of anything, anything at all that I've seen or heard that might mean anything to you. I've tried but I can't! Why won't you believe me?"

Alex and Bradley stepped forward. "No!" I shrieked. "I'm telling you the truth! Ask me as many specific questions as you want. Maybe I'll remember some tiny detail. I don't know, but I can't think of anything that I haven't told you that might matter!" Dear God let that buy me some time, I pleaded in my head.

Aton held up his hand, stopping the advance of his henchmen. He considered me like a bug under a microscope. I held his gaze, entreating with my eyes, hoping he'd buy it. "I am in no hurry to end our association," he said at last.

Alex was sent to fetch a chair and the bald vampire took up station across from me at the card table once again.

"Now, Miss Fletcher, tell me what you remember from the night Nigel was killed."

I started slowly, recalling as much detail as I could and making up shit where I felt it was needed. Nothing too significant, just little things to make it seem like I was trying hard to remember even the most insignificant detail.

We went over what Hazel and I had to eat and drink that day. What had we discussed? What happened when Jaeger had come to the door? The phone call from Leontine (ok, I sort of smoothed over some of my caustic comments. No need to recount those).

Time drug on as slowly as I could make it. I stuttered unnecessarily. I often paused, asking for a moment to be sure I was recalling things clearly. I even dared to ask for another drink and a trip to the bathroom.

"Please? I know it's been a very long time since you had such needs, but it's very uncomfortable and hard to concentrate when you have to go this badly."

Finally I convinced him to let me use the john. Tweedle Dee and Tweedle Dum escorted me down the short hallway. It was nearly impossible for all three of us to be in the hall at the say time. Fortunately they didn't want to come in with me.

Again there were no windows. Big surprise. I really did have to go and was very happy to be able to relieve myself and have access to a sink. I did my best to avoid looking in the mirror. Inside the medicine cabinet I found some toothpaste. It was an off brand and tasted like baking soda but at least my teeth felt better after I'd scrubbed them with some paste on my finger.

Closing the cabinet, I caught a glimpse of my face. Not much, just a bit, but I could see my skin was gray. Literally, the horrible gray coloring of a corpse. I didn't need to know that. I hunched over the sink ready to hurl up my two glasses of water and any traces of toothpaste. Mercifully, it didn't come, but a knock came on the door instead. "Be right out!" I called. Taking as deep a breath as I could manage, I splashed some water on my face, ran my hands over my hair and left the bathroom.

My silent escorts followed me back to the bedroom. Bradley blocked my view of whatever lay beyond. All I could see were the tops of blank walls of another room beyond the hall.

Reluctantly, I took my seat opposite my captor and steeled myself for another round of questions.

"What happened after Angel broke down the door?"

"He asked if I was ok. I told him that I thought that I was. I wasn't really sure, I was so shaken up and Leontine had beaten the crap out of me." The bastard smiled when I said that.

"Did you suffer any serious injuries?"

"Nothing too serious, no, surprisingly. I had some cuts and a great many bruises. I hurt like hell all over. I suppose I might have had a minor concussion or something, but I never got checked out."

"I see," he replied not bothering to hide his disappointment. "Go on. What happened next?"

"Angel saw Leontine on the floor and he, uh, well, he did what vampires do." I hoped that would be sufficient. Aton didn't interject, so I went on. I left the room and went into the kitchen. I splashed water on my face and washed my hands."

"Did you notice anything? Was anyone else in the house? Did you hear anything?"

I pretended to be thinking hard. "No, I couldn't see anyone else. The house is really small. Unless someone was hiding in the bedrooms. The doors were closed. Except for Angel in the back room, everything was quiet."

It had been very quiet. I didn't have to work hard to remember that. It was the most quiet 'quiet' I had ever known. Nothing had ever been so quiet. No bugs, no cars, no people, no wind. No nothing. No signs of life of any kind anywhere. It seemed as if the entire planet had gone still. It was eerie.

"I went out the front door," I continued. "It was so dark and so still. I couldn't hear anything and I didn't see anyone. I called out to Hazel and Jaeger but they didn't answer." Then I paused. Did I tell him what happened next? It would make it all more authentic, but would it anger him too much to hear it? I decided I had to be honest with this much at least. I had to make him believe it was *all* true, so I had to come clean with this part.

Shuddering, I said honestly "I don't know if you want to hear the next part." I lowered my eyes to indicate my pity for him. Apparently that splash of water did me some good. I'd made the right move. Aton shifted uncomfortably in his seat.

"Ridiculous! What could you possibly have to say that would upset me?"

I nodded at him sadly, maintaining the pity posture. "Ok, if you're sure." I paused for dramatic effect, taking a deep breath, I went on "I saw something shiny over on the side of the yard and I went towards it. It was a, a body." I paused again, swallowing hard and looking up at Aton under my lashes. "It was," I nodded and shrugged indicating that it was Nigel's body.

"I need no protecting from you, human! I have seen more dead bodies than you have seen alive!"

"I'm sorry. It's just that I know you cared for him a great deal and I can't imagine it would be easy to hear such things. But maybe that's just because I'm human and I view death differently than you do. I was trying to be respectful." Would he buy it? I held my breath and looked scared. That wasn't too difficult to do.

He continued to glare at me, nostrils flaring, but at a slightly less hostile level. I wasn't sure if that meant he was buying the humble thing or what, but I'd take what I could get.

"So then Lily showed up," I continued, "and said that she had been sent to bring me to Darius. I had never met her before. She told me to hold her hands and trust her and then we, I don't know what it's called, we sort of transported somehow to the mansion,"

"Wait a moment. You traveled with the faerie? Through use of her magic?"

Oh crap! I didn't know that was a big deal. "Yeah. Is that important?"

Aton ignored my question. He sat forward and peered at me more intently. "Tell me how it was done."

"I, I don't know how. She just asked me if I trusted her and told me to hold onto her hands. Oh, she had me close my eyes. Is that important?"

"What else did she do?"

"Umm, nothing. Well, I don't know. My eyes were closed and she was holding my hands. I felt the ground go out from under my feet and I was afraid I was going to fall but she just told me to hang on and that I was going to be fine. I felt air moving around me and then we sort of landed and I opened my eyes and we were inside the mansion."

"Did she say anything, any special words? An incantation? Did she use any objects?"

Damn! Poker face, Hero, poker face! "No, nothing. Just what I said, about trusting her and to hang on. It was pitch black out, but I didn't see anything and she didn't appear to have anything when we landed in the mansion."

I could tell he wasn't completely sure he believed me but he urged me to go on. I told him about her letting them know we had arrived and sitting down to wait. Oh crap! He had known so many things already, would he know about her taking me out of the anteroom to clean the blood off of me? Shit! I'd have to own up to that one and play as dumb as I could.

"Tell me exactly how she did it, leave nothing out," Aton ordered.

Nodding, I pretending to be working hard to remember each tiny detail, when in fact, the entire ordeal was firmly embedded in my brain in glorious Technicolor.

"She had a bag or purse or something and she took something out of it. I couldn't see what it was, she held it in her hand. Then she waved her hand over me and quietly mumbled something in a language I didn't understand. It was sort of under her breath, I couldn't really tell anything she was saying. My skin felt all prickly and itchy and I wanted to scratch. Then when she was done she put whatever it was back in her bag and the blood was all gone."

"You didn't ask her how she managed to do it?"

I shook my head. "I had just fought for my life and nearly killed someone. Then had a vampire come in and finish her off. A vampire, I might add, that I had only found out a few days before really existed. By the time I had travelled by magic to a mansion filled with vampires and realized I was covered in blood, I really didn't care how the blood got off of me. And I was tired and sore and beyond caring how magic worked at that point." For once I was telling him the God's honest truth.

"You have no idea what was in her bag or what she had in her hand?"

Again I shook my head. "I couldn't see anything."

"And you didn't think to ask?"

"No, I didn't. Under other circumstances maybe I would have but not then, not after everything that had happened. I didn't care. All I knew was she was one of the good guys and was looking out for me. Why? What's so important about cleaning my clothes up?"

He sat back in his chair. Clearly he hadn't intended for me to realize this part of the conversation was so significant. I must have done a really good job of convincing him that I was stupid if he didn't think I was going to pick up on that. "Tell me what happened next."

I told him about seeing Darius, as much as he needed to know. Then I told him about going to see Hazel. I figured he knew about all of this so there was no sense in trying to hide it.

"Did you notice anything unusual while you were visiting the faerie Hazel?"

"Everything was unusual! I'm a human. Her wounds were horrible but she laughed and said not to worry, that she'd be fine by morning. I felt so terrible knowing she was hurt like that because of me."

"And the Healer?"

"Oh, yeah. The tall guy. He came in and gave her something to drink."

"What did he give her?"

"I don't know. It wasn't my place to ask such things and he didn't say what it was."

"What did it look like? What type of container was it in?"

I shrugged. "I don't know. I went over to the corner to get out of his way. I was behind him while he tended to her. I didn't see what he gave her. Wait! I think I remember when she was drinking it I saw a little flash of something, like a reflection. I think maybe whatever it was in might have been crystal. I'm not sure."

I could feel the anger building up inside him again. "You could see nothing? Nothing?!"

My eyes were like saucers and I slid down in my chair cowering. "I felt so bad about her being hurt. I just wanted to get out of the doctor's way so he could help her. I didn't know anyone was going to want to know what he gave her!" I cried.

Now, I know what I said earlier about how if someone was torturing me I'd give them what they wanted right off; that I couldn't see anything worth suffering for. But... I

94

really don't have any idea what divulging the secrets of the faeries magic stones might mean for them, and I don't just mean Hazel and Lily, I mean the whole faerie race. I was terrified of being bitten again. I sure as hell didn't want to die and I certainly didn't want to be a vampire either, but I wasn't going to give up the faeries if I felt I had any chance of getting out of this without it.

Half my body was under the flimsy card table. The rest was barely hanging on to the chair. Aton loomed over me on the verge of rage.

"Perhaps," he began in a strange high pitched voice, "Alex can jog your memory for you?"

As Alex leapt forward for me I dove the rest of the way under the table. The table went flying and I scrambled around on all fours trying to avoid the blonde vampire. Loudly I screamed "No! There's nothing to remember! I'd tell you, I would, I would!"

Seeing as the card table was the only cover in the tiny room filled with me and three vampires, I didn't really have any place to go. I was hauled to my feet, none too gently, and thrown against the wall. Alex pinned my arms straight from my sides. "No, no, please don't," I begged as he leaned his head in. I tried to block his approach with my chin and move my head around to keep him from my neck, but it was no good. He was too strong.

I saw colored spots before my eyes from the pain of slamming my head back against the wall when he sunk his fangs into me. The pain from the bite made the colors run. Had I not been so afraid and in so much pain, the artist in me would have appreciated the effect.

'Dear God, please just let me die.' I prayed silently to myself. I figured he owned me that much. Just let me die. I could feel myself slipping out of consciousness. A prayer from childhood rang in my head.

"Now I lay me down to sleep.

I pray the Lord my soul to keep.

If I should die before I wake

I pray the Lord my soul to take."

Funny, as I child I never really realized what a horribly morbid prayer that is, especially for children to recite. Leave it to me though, to have something as pointless as that be my last thought before passing out.

Chapter 8

White. Everything was a sea of white. Was I dead? Was this Heaven? I waited to see or hear or feel something that would indicate my place in the universe.

After a few moments of silence I decided that if this was Heaven, it was sorely lacking. Therefore, I was probably alive. I hate to admit it, but I wasn't sure I was happy with that realization. Death was sadly looking like the better choice of the two.

Again I lay still on the crappy little bed and again I was afraid to move; afraid of what I might feel or what I might not feel. Stop, Hero! Don't think of those things, think of something else. Sure, like what day was it? Was it night time, morning? Was anyone looking for me?

Actually, I'd tried not to think about that too much. Naturally my mind had wandered there a few times during the brief time I'd had without my pal Aton in the room, but it made me too anxious to think about. I still had no idea how they managed to get past Jaeger. Was he hurt, was he alive? What about Hazel? I had been taken at her home. Did they do anything to her to keep her quiet? One way or another, Darius would know I had been captured. Would he care? Would he consider he had done his duty, especially if his Hunter had been lost or injured in the process? And Kin, did he even know? Where was he? Had he tried to call me? Phone reception was so iffy wherever it was he was at. He might not even know anything had happened to me.

What about my friends? After having to leave my home and stay first with Kin and then with Hazel if I suddenly just disappeared would they think I've just taken off with a new friend again? Will they be worried or just be angry? No, I knew my friends better than that. They'd be worried.

In a repeat of yesterday's events, or what I thought of as yesterday anyway, I lay in the bed with silent tears running down the sides of my face. I was probably going to die here and no one would know it. God only knows what the vampires would do with my body. I'd just be another missing person statistic; another cold case file to entertain the masses.

Unless they decided to make me a vampire. Well, actually, as far as my friends were concerned, the results would be the same. I'd be dead to them. A loved one who disappeared mysteriously and was never heard from again. I shivered, nauseated at the idea of being made vampire, of belonging to Aton for all eternity.

Whoa! Wait a minute! I sat bolt upright on the bed. When Kin had been explaining vampire government and politics to me he had said that Darius required vampires to request permission to make new vampires in his sector. Ok, Hero, calm down. My mind was running one hundred miles an hour. Too many thoughts to sift through at once.

I got up from the bed and began to walk slowly around the room, the physical activity helping me to pace the bustle in my brain.

So Aton couldn't make me a vampire without Darius' say so. Although, I suppose Aton might be one of those vampires that doesn't care about authority and does what he pleases, figuring he'll never get caught. All right, so where did that leave me? Dead, that's where it left me. If Aton had gone to Darius about me then surely someone would have saved me by now, wouldn't they? I mean, Darius wouldn't bother having Jaeger look out for me if he was just going to let Aton turn me or kill me.

Crap! I didn't know! I softly banged my head against the wall. Well, I didn't know for a fact what Darius would do, but I had to assume Darius had not been approached for approval to change me. It just made the most sense. Maybe I wanted it to make the most sense, but either way, that was what I was going with.

So I was looking at death. I started to shake and my legs went out from under me. Folding onto the floor in a pathetic heap, I sobbed quietly, trying not to let the vampires outside my room hear me. Ironic isn't it? Only a few short minutes ago I was hoping I was dead.

What could I do? How could I get out of this? Even if I decided to come clean and tell Aton about the bloodstone what were the odds that he would let me go now? Not good. Non-existent, actually.

Think! Think! I had to find a way to make myself valuable; to be worth more alive than dead. But how? I had no idea, but I knew if I came up with an idea, I wouldn't like it.

I wanted to rail at God again for screwing with me so much, but I just couldn't. I was too scared, too weak and too much in hope that He'd intervene and save me. As a general rule it's not a good idea to bitch at the guy you're hoping will save you, especially when that guy is the Lord Almighty.

I crawled over to the bed and hoisted myself up onto it, curling into the fetal position as soon as I lifted my legs up off the floor.

"Mom," I said softly, "if you can hear me, please, please help me. Be my guardian angel and help me get out of here. Whisper in my ear and tell me what to do. Or get an angel to smite the vampires or something, but please, Mom, I need you."

My eyes were closed tightly, tears seeping out of the corners. No whisper came. No signs of smiting, whatever they might be, appeared to be coming from the other room. So, I took a deep breath and steadied myself. You're on your own, Hero. It was time to think of a plan.

I heard them approach this time. They made no effort to be quiet. Either they assumed I would be sleeping again or just didn't care. I remained on the bed, where I'd been lying and planning for some time, and pretended I hadn't heard them.

"Time to get up, Miss Fletcher."

I sat up and swung my legs over the side of the bed so I was facing Aton. I met his gaze, but said nothing.

"Tsk tsk. You look terrible. You really must take better care of yourself." He was greatly amused by his rotten remarks.

"I'll keep that in mind," I replied flatly. "I don't suppose that means you are going to offer me anything to eat or drink?"

"Sorry," he said. "We're all out."

I grinned ruefully. "So, what's it going to be today?"

"The same, Miss Fletcher. Nothing has changed. I want you to tell me the truth."

Rubbing my hands over my face, I sighed heavily. When I lifted my head, there were tears in my eyes once again. "Just kill me. Please."

The bald vampire was taken aback. Clearly, he had not expected this. "Kill you, Miss Fletcher, really,"

But I didn't let him finish. "I know you're going to kill me. Darius would never give you permission to turn me and there's no way you'd let me go after all of this and I really have told you everything I know. I can't take any more. Please, just kill me. End this, please." I was sobbing, rocking back and forth on the edge of the bed.

My attitude confused him. "Darius has nothing to do with this!"

"I may not know a lot about vampires, but I do know that Darius has to give his permission for any new vampires to be created in his territory."

"I care nothing for what Darius wants!"

"What?" I said in surprise, looking at Aton in wonder. "You'd really go against Darius like that?"

"I am older than he. I reside in another sector. His rules, his laws, they are meaningless to me."

"Oh, then no wonder."

"No wonder what?"

"No wonder you would defeat his number one man, take a human that was under his explicit protection and do the things you've done. This isn't really about me or Nigel at all is it?"

"What are you talking about? You make no sense?"

"This is all a red herring. You're looking for a reason to try and overthrow Darius!" I announced, clapping my hands to my cheeks in awe and amazement. "You think if you can find some reason to trace Nigel's demise back to a fault of Darius' you can challenge him and take over his territory!"

The wheels in his mind were spinning so fast you could hear them whine. Alex and Bradley were looking at Aton with even more admiration than they usually displayed so revoltingly.

Aton's eyes darted quickly between me and his vamp henchmen. Seeing that we all believed it could be true, that he could be capable of such a coup, he decided to grab hold of the brass ring I'd offered.

"You are more clever than I gave you credit for," he said at last.

Yes! He'd taken the bait. Now to reel him in. I had to do it gently; I had to give him enough line to trap himself with.

"That's why you wanted me. You knew I didn't know anything about Mike all along. You just hoped I'd tell you something you could use against Darius. That's why you were so concerned with how I got to the mansion and all that." Then I stood quickly and dramatically, thrusting out my arm and pointing at him. "If you think you can use me as a hostage, as a bargaining chip!" I didn't finish the sentence; I just shook my head and pretended to sob.

A smug grin curled the corner of Aton's mouth. "And what makes you think you'd be worth bargaining? A human?"

I made a show of averting his gaze and seeming guilty. My God he was easy to fool. He must really have a low opinion of humans to not realize he was being played.

"But," he started slowly, pausing to walk closer to me. "He *did* have his very best man watching you, didn't he? And he did negotiate with Ilderim for your safety. You must have *some* value."

He nodded to Alex and Bradley and in an instant they were gone and the lock was being turned in the door. I was suddenly alone again.

Lowering myself to the bed, I let out a long, slow breath. Well, if there was one thing I'd learned about vampires and supernatural creatures; most of them are very vain, most of them love and want power and most of them vastly underestimate humans. Thank God!

103

It had been a complete guess on my part that Aton would feel he deserved to be a Magistrate. I knew he was extremely old, even for a vampire. The reaction of other vampires at the news of him investigating Nigel's death proved he was feared and respected. I was counting on his having the same overblown self-image and inflated sense of entitlement as some of the other older vampires I'd met since I started dating Kin.

Ok, so deflecting Aton's sense of revenge onto Darius may not seem like a nice thing to do, but, I was trying to save my life. And let's face it, Darius has a whole hell of a lot better chance of surviving a battle with Aton than I do.

As I lay down on the bed and made myself comfortable, I couldn't help thinking how easily Aton grasped on to the idea of usurping Darius. In my mind I thought of the old Bugs Bunny cartoon where he is a matador. Remember? He thinks he's beaten the bull and he stands there at the door making all those bad puns. What a nin-cow-poop, what a gulla-bull! At least I could still smile and find humor. That was a good sign. A very good sign.

I didn't have long to rest on my laurels. My vampire companions were soon back.

"Come on," said Bradley, motioning toward the door.

"Where?" I asked as I stood. He didn't answer, he just pointed toward the open door.

I stepped out into the hallway where Alex was waiting. He took me by the arm and led me through the main room of what appeared to be an apartment. Might have been a condo. It was hard to tell, we were moving so quickly.

With barely enough time to register that there was a large rectangular room with a covered up basement level window, I was out of the apartment and in yet another hallway. It smelled damp and dirty.

Bradley was right behind us as Alex ushered me through the door opposite and into a parking garage. The smell in there was even worse. It smelled of garbage and exhaust and Heaven knows what.

A large black sedan stood a few feet away, its rear door open. I was shoved through the door and nearly landed face first in Aton's lap. He thrust out his hand to stop me, thankfully, though I wasn't happy about the contact just the same. The door was shut behind me and in a flash Alex and Bradley were in the front seat and the sedan was on the move. Aton was not wasting any time.

"Where are you taking me?" I asked, hoping for, but not expecting, an answer.

"To see a friend," he replied cryptically.

Friend? Whose friend? His friend, my friend? I tried to just settle into the seat and be grateful for the fact that I was out of that room and hadn't been bitten again. Though I was so tired, weak, hungry and thirsty, that I didn't know how much longer I could care about much of anything.

The rear windows of the vehicle were darkly tinted. More darkly than I thought was legal anymore, but it also seemed to be an older car. Perhaps there was some loophole about that. I could see vaguely where we were, but things were not very sharp or distinct. It appeared to be around twilight or perhaps it was just overcast. Even out of the windshield, which was not tinted, there wasn't much light, but I didn't notice the streetlights or many headlights on.

I tried, unsuccessfully, to determine where we were. I was so weak and tired from hunger and loss of blood I just couldn't make my brain process that quickly passing scenery. We were closer to the city, I could tell that much easily. We were not in suburbia anymore, Toto.

Finally, I just rested my forehead against the cool glass and closed eyes. If I was sitting in the back seat without a blindfold or anything, then where I'd been couldn't be important. It was where we were going that mattered and I hadn't a clue.

The chill of the glass felt good against my skin. Not that I'd been warm, but it was nice just to feel something new, something familiar and something not painful. My mind focused on the soft hum of the moving car and the gentle sway back and forth that enveloped me like a warm blanket. They were also familiar and comforting; the things of long drives through New Hampshire and Maine as a child with my family in the summers. Driving for hours to get to remote cabins and chalets my father would rent for vacation.

I tried to imagine it was the old Crown Victoria station wagon I was inside now and not the black sedan. In my head, it was William beside me and my parents in the front seat silently enjoying the view as we travelled through the White Mountains. What lovely memories. How many times did my father make us get out to look at the Old Man? How many picnics had we had at the falls in Franconia Notch? If I lived through this, I vowed I would take a trip there again, even if the Old Man had fallen.

I had cried when that happened. Does that surprise you? That someone like me would cry over a pile of rocks falling off a mountain? Well, I did. It made me sad to think that I'd never take my own children to see that wonder now. We have so few things left in the world to remind us to wonder at the things created by Nature and not by Man.

Ok, this was taking a bad turn. I opened my eyes and looked out the window again, hoping to divert myself from sad thoughts. Not easy under the circumstances. We were definitely moving away from Boston, but I still didn't recognize where we were.

My three companions were completely still. They hadn't spoken and they hadn't moved a muscle. I think perhaps in some ways it's incredibly boring to be a vampire. But then again, at least they are comfortable with silence.

We turned off into a decidedly residential area and my heart began to beat even faster than it had been. Where were we going? The sedan made its way through several narrow streets and tight turns; traveling down roads that were built long before anyone had conceived of things such as automobiles.

At last we turned down a street that was slightly wider than the tiny roads we'd squeezed through, though there was so much dirt on the road it took a moment to be sure it was paved underneath. It was lined on both sides with dense woods and brush. I noticed a wooden sign nailed to a tree pointing in the direction we were headed. It read "Céad míle fáilte romhat!" And no, I haven't the foggiest idea how to say it or what it means.

The trees gave way to a clearing and soon we found ourselves coming upon a quaint little cottage, complete with thatched roof. I had a very sick feeling.

The sedan stopped a couple of yards away from a beat up SUV. Its blue paint was marred with dings and scratches and the front bumper looked as though it had been banged out more than once.

Aton lowered his window and a large man, vampire presumably, approached. "Is everything as I requested?" Aton asked. The tall, dark-skinned vampire merely bowed. Ick! I hated that subservient crap. "Good. Bring her here."

Her? Oh holy crap! I didn't want to know who 'her' was.

The dark-skinned vampire returned in an instant along with another vampire even darker and larger that he was. Between them was a tiny little woman with white hair. She was in ancient iron shackles on her wrists and ankles and there were heavy chains looped over her shoulders and across her chest like a pair of bandoleers. I was amazed she could stand beneath the weight of them. If that weren't bad enough, she had a large dirty rag tied around her head, firmly implanted in her mouth to keep her quiet.

"Oh, Lily, no!" I cried.

"Silence!" Aton bellowed with an angry stare. "Sit back and be quiet!"

They brought Lily up to the open window. "Well, well, what have we here?" Aton said gleefully as he reached beneath the edge of Lily's fuchsia tunic and fiercely yanked her bag of stones breaking the chord that secured them around her waist.

Despite the gag Lily cried out in agony as her stones were taken from her. It was gut-wrenching. Had I been allowed to eat or drink I was sure I would have been ill then and I took pleasure in the knowledge that I would have vomited all over Aton.

Aton jerked his head toward me and said "Put her in the other side." Before I had a chance to scoot over Lily was being shoved in beside me.

"I'm so sorry," I mouthed at we adjusted ourselves in the back seat.

We wasted no time turning around and heading back down the long road that had led to Lily's cottage. "Where are we going now?" I asked.

That cold, cruel smile was back. His black eyes twinkled as he replied "Oh, it is a surprise. You would not want me to ruin the surprise, now would you?" He chuckled malevolently as he settled back into his seat.

Chapter 9

I longed to talk to Lily, but Aton had made it quite clear we weren't even to look at one another, let alone speak. Out of the corner of my eye I could see the heavy iron shackles on her wrists that must have been hundreds of years old. They were rusted and encrusted with years' worth of God-knows-what. Lily's thin, pale arms looked as though they would snap under the weight of them. Her misery radiated off of her in palpable waves. And I had thought I could feel no worse.

What had I done? How had they found Lily and gotten to her so quickly? Did Aton have a spy in the faerie clan? I had assumed he knew I was at Hazel's because someone had followed me there, but what if I was wrong? I was so confused. The lack of food and drink and little sleep was taking its toll, not to mention being damn low on blood. It was hard to focus, hard to make my mind follow any one train of thought.

What about Lily's stones? Had that been my fault? Surely a vampire as old as Aton had been aware of the faeries' use of stones for ages. I was sure Hazel and Lily hadn't tried to hide their stones or the use of them. Hadn't they said to me that vampires knew about the stones but not which stone did what or what exactly they were capable of doing with the stones? Still, I couldn't help feeling it was all my fault.

It was getting dark and visibility within the confines of the dark sedan was murky. Carefully, I inched my right arm back slowly so that my right hand was next to Lily's manacled left hand, and in the low light of the back seat I hazarded

110

extending my little finger and linking it with hers. It was a small gesture, but even that miniscule amount of contact and defiance was comforting and reassuring. I felt Lily respond as well. She squeezed her little finger around mine. The nearest thing to a hug two terrified friends could manage under such dire circumstances.

I had given up caring where we were going. I didn't even want to think about it. After all, what did it matter? Nothing good was going to happen when we got wherever we were going. Knowing ahead of time wouldn't change it and I was all out of clever ideas.

Yes, I was feeling sorry for myself. Wouldn't you? Give me a break, ok? I think we can all agree it was a little hard to feel hopeful in such a situation. Having Lily beside me was bittersweet really. We've already explored the guilt side of the equation, but on the other side, it was nice to no longer be alone. Perhaps that was selfish of me, I don't know, but I think it's fair to say most of us would feel the same.

We drove and drove. I can't say how long or even to where. I was too much inside my own head, trying to ignore my fear, my hunger, thirst, guilt and half a dozen other things. It might have been twenty minutes or it might have been an hour, but when we finally arrived at our destination, both Lily and I were weary and worse for the wear.

I tried not to look at Lily as we pulled into the large estate. Really, I did. My own natural reflex was so strong and my guard so weak that I forgot and turned to her in time to see a glimmer of recognition before I remembered Aton's warning and quickly darted my eyes forward to make it look as though I had been looking at the building and not at Lily. Thank goodness for the darkness.

But I had seen her expression. She knew where we were. Forcing myself to see the glass as half full, I determined that this would be a good thing. I wasn't certain what was awaiting us inside but there was a chance, no matter how remote, that Lily's knowledge of this place and its inhabitants might help us.

We drove through a gate and down a long drive to the back of a large estate house. There had been a few houses visible up on the main road, but now we were secluded and shielded from the view of the road. There was no way neighbors or passersby would notice anything going on here unless the place were engulfed in flames.

The black sedan came to a halt and a troop of armored men and women circled us. A large man with bulging muscles and way too much facial hair stepped forward. He had a large automatic weapon of some kind in his hands and he didn't look as though he'd mind using it. (Sorry, I'm no good with guns and weaponry. I know what a revolver looks like and the rest are guns, rifles etc. That's as detailed as I get).

Facial Hair Guy motioned to Alex who was in the driver's seat. Slowly, Alex unfolded himself from the front seat, his hands up. "Aton comes to see Ilderim as a friend," he said.

Ilderim! This was the home of Leontine's Menagerie? Ugh! Talk about adding insult to injury! But from what Kin had said, Ilderim was a very fair leader. Maybe he wouldn't want to see us hurt and he would probably not want to see Darius overthrown in favor of a hot head like Aton.

"He was not expecting you," replied the Hairy One. "Wait here." He spoke quietly to another armed guard who had been behind him. This new guard took up post with his own automatic weapon while his superior took off to notify Ilderim of our arrival.

Alex lowered his hands and the guard cautioned "Un uh. You don't want to do that. Keep them where I can see them."

I couldn't see Alex's face, but I could imagine his reaction. I heard him reply "You know guns don't hurt vampires."

The guard grinned widely. "They do if the bullets are wooden."

That got Aton's attention. He rolled down his window.

"Don't try anything," said a female guard, stepping forward and pointing her weapon at Aton.

"I would not think of it, my dear. I merely wanted to ask why on earth you would be armed with wooden bullets. Has something happened? I was not aware that your menagerie was at war with anyone."

"We aren't," said the male guard, "but we are always prepared, especially when there are rogue vampires in the area." He said this last part as menacingly as he could manage. After a couple of days with Aton, he would really have had to bring it to even register on the menacing meter. Needless to say, he failed. It came out sounding lame and Aton let him know.

"Rogue, aha," he stopped to chuckle, "rogue vampires! Oh! Oh my! That, ha ha!" he chuckled some more, "oh that really is rich!"

I have to say I don't think I have ever wanted to slap someone so hard in my life, and that's really saying something. I was glad the backseat was still relatively dark and that Aton's attention was turned in the opposite direction so he couldn't see the look on my face. Yeah, yeah, I know. Self-control, blah, blah, blah. Well, sometimes you just can't. Sometimes a look just happens. This was one of those times.

"Well, what do you call it when vampires from another territory come and break laws and openly disrespect the Magistrate?" asked the female guard. I was beginning to like her.

"I call it a misunderstanding."

She raised her eyebrow, indicating she clearly thought his response was total BS.

Before things could escalate, the guy with the hirsute chin was back. "Ilderim will receive you, Aton. Your men will wait here."

"And what of my prisoners? Will you see they are properly housed?"

The guard looked past him through the window. "The human?" he asked.

"Yes, and a friend."

The guard walked around to the other side of the car and opened the door next to Lily. "A faerie!" he muttered in surprise. After selecting two other guards to take us to lockup and issuing them their orders, Facial Hair Guy motioned for Aton to go ahead of him.

As I watched them walk away and into the grand house I wanted to yell 'Help me! Get me out of here!' but I knew that would be stupid. After all, look at how Leontine had felt about humans. Why should I expect any of these guards to feel sorry for me?

Lily and I climbed out of the car. I was now free to help my friend and speak to her and make contact. The guards didn't care. "Come on, Lily, lean on me," I told her as we started our trek towards our new prison.

"This way," said a sandy-haired guard. He was small compared to the other guards, but well-built. His bright green eyes made me think of Kin. Oh! Where was Kin?

The other guard, an older Latino man with long graying hair, followed behind. We were led to a door with a large circle door pull where the handle would be and huge ornate hinges. It looked like something out of an old movie. I expected it to open onto a dungeon, but it opened onto a clean, modern, brightly lit staircase.

Down we went into the basement, along a cold, yellowish corridor to a series of rooms with heavy doors with small windows in them. Lockup. They put us together in the first room. I was thankful they didn't separate us.

"Can we have some water?" I asked as we filed into the room.

"I will ask," replied the sandy-haired guard.

They left us there sitting on hard stone benches, awaiting our fate. As soon as I heard their footsteps fade I got up and went to Lily and removed the gag from around her head.

"Oh, Lily, you poor thing! I am so, so sorry!"

"Oh," she moaned. She tried to rub her hands over her sore mouth but the ancient contraption about her wrists made it almost impossible.

I brushed the hair off of her face and tried my best to soothe her while I choked back tears. "These things," I said pointing at the shackles and chains, "they do more to you than just confine you, don't they?"

She nodded weakly. "They drain my magic. Keep me from performing spells," the little faerie gasped. "Oh, my stones!" she cried pitifully, barely able to squeak.

My heart broke for her. I wanted to say something comforting, but there was nothing to be said. So I just sat next to her and pulled her head onto my shoulder and wrapped my arms around her. It was all I could do.

"Oh, if only we could get word to Darius," I sighed.

"Darius?" Lily asked feebly.

I began to tell her of my great idea to get myself free and how I put Darius in the thick of it without him knowing when we heard a noise.

116

The door opened to reveal the sandy-haired guard. He signaled me to be quiet, then came in and shut the door behind him.

"Here," he whispered, handing me canteen. I took it and sipped the most delicious thing I'd ever tasted. It was so cold and sweet and wet! Nice and wet! I felt so relieved and marginally better. I was still hungry and tired and weak, but it was a start. I took another drink and then offered the canteen to Lily.

She had drifted off too. "Here, Lily, drink." The little faerie lifted her head just enough to get the container to her mouth. Barely had the liquid passed her lips when her eyes opened like saucers.

"Nectar!" She stared first at me and then she noticed the guard for the first time. "Buckthorne!"

"Shh!" he cautioned. "It's only a quarter nectar. Any more than that and they'll smell it, even with the cap on."

"Blackthorne, take these off of me, please," begged Lily presenting her hands to him.

His eyes filled with tears. "I'm sorry, I can't. I wasn't even supposed to bring you the water you asked for."

"Ilderim denied us water?"

"No," he said shaking his head. "Aton. You are his prisoners and only he can dictate what you can and cannot have."

"Then why are you defying him?" I asked.

He drew a great shaking breath and exhaled slowly. I thought he might be ill. I looked questioningly at Lily, but she just shrugged. "Because it is my fault you are here."

"How is it your fault that I'm here?" I asked.

"Forgive me. Not you. You," he said, clearly addressing himself to Lily.

Lily and Blackthorne looked into each other's eyes. "No," Lily gasped, almost a whisper. "Oh, no, you didn't? Why?"

Blackthorne sat back and turned his head from us. "Eight months ago, I fell in love with a shifter. She turns into a doe. A lovely, sweet, delicate looking doe. She kept coming to the brook by my home and I didn't realize she was a shifter at first. I began to look forward to seeing her. She was so pretty and it had been ages since I had seen wild deer in the area. Then one day, as she approached the brook, she resumed her human form. Needless to say, I was surprised. But she was just as lovely and graceful as a human as she had been as a doe. We fell in love."

I looked at Lily and rolled my eyes. Seriously? We needed a big dramatic love story now? Just tell us what the hell happened?

"I came to live here at the menagerie so I could be with her all the time. Most of the people are really nice here."

"But?" I prompted when he didn't continue.

He looked sheepishly at us. "But some of the people here are not so nice. You learned that," he said, looking pointedly at me.

I certainly had. "Go on," I said.

"Well, Leontine," he said, looking at me again, "did you ever wonder how she got Hazel's number and found out where she lived?"

"Blackthorne, you didn't! How could you!" cried Lily.

"Because she threatened to kill Delia!" he sobbed, reaching out to Lily with pleading hands. "I didn't know Hero. She was a stranger who meant nothing to me. I'm sorry, but it's the truth. I didn't know the details of the situation at the time. Naturally, Leontine made it sound as though Hero had done something horrible and had to be taken care of for the safety of the whole menagerie. But even had I known it was for something so petty, how could you expect me to risk the life of someone I love for a stranger?"

"Hazel isn't a stranger!"

"She said she just wanted the human. She said no harm would come to Hazel."

"Ha! And you believed her?" Lily spat.

"What was I supposed to do?"

"You should have gone to Ilderim," I suggested.

"Do you think I didn't think of that?" he questioned, turning to me. "She had me cornered. Nigel had Delia somewhere and was waiting for the signal from Leontine. If I hadn't told her what she wanted to know right then and there…" He began to cry.

Lily and I looked at one another. We didn't know whether to pity him or think him pathetic. "You had magic you could have utilized, Blackthorne. There were things you could have done. Even if you had felt you had no choice at that moment, you could have gone to Ilderim or even Darius right away."

The male faerie snuffled and wiped his nose on the back of his hand. Well, apparently that disgusting masculine behavior isn't restricted to humans. "I did go to Ilderim, but I waited too long. By the time I was given an audience the fight was over."

"Well, Leontine's dead. Who made you betray Lily and how? Surely after what Leontine did Ilderim would have made it clear that you and Delia were off limits?" Actually, I didn't know what the head of the menagerie would or wouldn't do, but it seemed like common sense to me.

Blackthorne nodded. "Delia was returned to me. She was…," he paused, searching for the right words. "She was, um, not harmed in any obvious way. Not in any way that she could prove Nigel had done, but he had his own methods of inflicting pain." The faerie winced at the memory of those methods. I was glad he didn't describe them. I'd experienced enough of vampire torture methods recently. I didn't need to hear about any extra special ones. "But when I was approached this time, I was told they had my sister captive."

120

"Mari!" Lily gasped.

"Yes," he croaked. "I do not know where she is or who has her."

"Well, who is making you give them information?" I couldn't help asking.

Nervously, Blackthorne looked over his shoulder at the door. "I can't say his name. I shouldn't even be here now. There are vampires in the menagerie. They might hear us."

He stood and went to the door. "Wait a minute!" I called in a stage whisper. He jumped back from the door, afraid of being caught.

"Shh!" the faerie cautioned needlessly.

"You still have your bag of stones," I announced, pointing at the battered pouch hanging out from under his tunic. "You can use your magic to get us out of here."

"No, I can't," he snapped. "This is a cell!" he stated unnecessarily. "Precautions have been taken against using magic in here."

"Then take us to where you can use it!" I demanded. I was sick of this guy. I felt bad for the position he was in, but really! If he had gone to Ilderim and told him what had happened with Leontine and Nigel then no one else would have had a chance to pull this crap on him again. The rest of us should not have to keep paying because he was weak and stupid. Ok, maybe that was harsh, but I wasn't exactly feeling in a generous mood, all things considered.

As I'm sure you can guess he began to protest but I wasn't going to give in easily. He was the reason Leontine had found and nearly killed me. That led to the battle where Mike staked Nigel which led to me being kidnapped and him selling out Lily. Yeah, yeah, I know. You're going to say he had to, what choice did he have? Well, he has magic at his disposal and powerful friends to help him. Do I have those things? No. Have I sold out my friends? No. Maybe it's apples and oranges; whatever, but it was still fruit.

"We wouldn't be here if it wasn't for you Blackthorne. Your sister wouldn't be in danger if not for you either. Now you have a chance to do something right. Do it! Or as soon as the guards come back I'm going to tell them you've been here and told us everything!"

"What?! No! Why, why would you…" he was panicking.

I could tell Lily wasn't completely sure this was the way to go, but she wasn't going to interfere either. I was grateful for that. "Blackthorne, please. The iron. I don't know how much longer I can take it," Lily pleaded, looking as frail as ever.

He fished around in his bag of stones and pulled out a bright blue one with flecks of black. "Here. I always carry an extra turquoise with me. Do you have anything I can use to put this around your neck?"

Her own turquoise and whatever stone she chose to wear at the moment had been torn off of her neck when she was captured. "She can have my chain," I offered. I was wearing a silver chain with a heart on it. "I can take the pendant off so it's not in the way."

As quickly as my tired fingers would allow, I took the piece of turquoise from Blackthorne which had a smooth, round hole in the center and strung it onto my silver chain and then carefully placed it around Lily's neck. As the cool stone rested against her skin just below her collar bone she sighed slightly.

"Will that help? It's not one of your stones?"

Lily nodded slowly. "It will help some. Gifts given in times of crisis; gifts given selflessly, with love; they have a unique power of their own."

"Oh! I had no idea! Here," I said as I pulled off my amethyst claddagh ring. "It's probably big for you but," I pushed the gold circle onto her thumb where it fit snugly, "there, that ought to do. Is amethyst a good stone? Will that help you?"

My faerie friend had tears in her eyes when she spoke. "Thank you, Hero. I can feel that this is special to you. There is a great deal of love and sentiment attached to this stone."

I blushed. "My grandmother gave that to me for my sixteenth birthday. It was the last birthday I had with her."

"Well," interjected Blackthorne, "between those two you should be..."

"What?" I pounced. "What should she be? All better? Look at her! She's still in shackles, iron shackles, and her stones are gone. You think those two stones from us are going to make her whole again?"

123

"Blackthorne, take us to Darius," pleaded Lily. "Please, we must see Darius before it's too late. He will help you get your sister back."

"How can he?" he asked tearfully.

"Trust me, Blackthorne. Just get us to where you can use your travel stone and get us to the Magistrate."

"Yes, please!" I chimed in, of course. You know I couldn't keep quiet. "I don't have time to go into it now, but things are going to be so much worse if we don't get to Darius in time."

He started shaking his head and backing toward the door, whimpering. I couldn't help thinking he must carry *all* of his stones in that bag.

"Look at my neck, Blackie," I said; pulling my hair aside so he could see the bite marks. I twisted my head so he could see they were on both sides. "Look at Lily. And just a couple of weeks ago I nearly died because of you! And some people did die or were really badly hurt. You owe me, pal! Now just how far do we have to go to be able to use your magic?"

"Ju-just to the top of the stairs," he snuffled.

"Are you kidding me? Even in her state Lily could throw a rock to the bottom of those stairs, and then you only need a couple of seconds to get us gone. Now open that door and let's go!"

"But if the guard comes back, if someone sees us…"

"Oh for Christ's sake! For all the time we've been arguing no one has come and we could have been long gone, do you realize that, you wimp? Let's go!? I held my hand out for the key.

He hesitated, looking first at Lily and then at me. "Oh, hell! I'm going to live to regret this, I just know it.!"

"Yeah, well. You get us to Darius and then I can take care of that for you."

Chapter 10

I don't go in for that 'damsel in distress' thing. I don't want some big macho idiot to come riding in and save the day, thank you very much. I like to take care of myself whenever possible. Now, of course I realize that there are times when I'm just going to have to admit that I need help and I sure as hell was in one of those situations now. But here's the thing, I was beginning to think I'd rather suffer a big-talking, machismo jerk wad than have to put up with He Who Has No Spine. I felt like smacking him just for general purposes.

He forked over the key without any further persuading. It was easy to see why he was such an obvious mark. Carefully, I opened the cell door just a crack and listened. We three all stood silent and still, afraid to breathe that we might miss some tiny sound that would indicate a guard in the hallway.

At last we dared to move and I signaled my companions to move forward. Lily's ankle restraints made a terrible racket. All our eyes went as big as saucers as we waited to see if the sound had alerted anyone of our escape. When no indication of discovery came, I whispered to Blackthorne "Take out the stone you need now and hold it in your hand. Then pick up Lily and carry her so her chains don't make any noise."

Blackthorne nodded and did as he was told. I still didn't like him. I had no use for weak men, but at least he had accepted I was calling the shots and he was doing as he was told. Once he had the stone securely in his fist he went to Lily and gently scooped her up. I helped her raise her arms and loop them around his neck, just to be safe. Then we crept into the hall.

Thank God for adrenaline. I think it was the only thing keeping me going. My rapidly beating heart and I skulked toward the staircase as quickly as I dared, making sure the faeries were right behind me. We paused at the bottom of the stairs to listen for voices or sounds of anyone approaching.

Lily and I looked at Blackthorne. "It s-s-sounds o-ok," he stammered.

I positioned myself beside him, grasping the hand beneath Lily's shoulder blades; the hand that held the stone. "Start the spell the very moment we're clear," I whispered.

My heart hammered in my chest as we climbed the stairs. I was terrified that we'd get to the top just to have someone standing there waiting for us. Aton, with his cold, cruel smile, enjoying the look of shock on our face.

Steady, Hero, steady. We can do this. Just a little farther. There were only a few more steps to go. Holy crap! Voices! We stopped dead, ugh, poor choice of words, we stopped and pressed ourselves against the wall, praying we wouldn't be seen.

After a horrific moment, the voices began to fade, indicating they were moving away from us. Once it was quiet and we could breathe again, I looked at Blackthorne with resolve. 'Three steps and then the spell," I said in a tiny voice as I grabbed the hand with the stone again.

"Ready?" He nodded. "Ok, one, two, three!" We bounded up the last three steps and immediately Blackthorne began the spell. I stepped directly in front of him and grabbed his other hand. I didn't know if it was required, but I figured it wouldn't hurt.

He murmured and chanted feverishly and at first I was afraid it wasn't working. Were Lily's iron restraints affecting him too? And then it happened. I began to feel the ground go out from beneath me and my hair whip around my face. We were travelling. We would be safe now. I very nearly cried.

Then, over Blackthorne's chanting, I heard shouting. Many voices shouting. I wanted to open my eyes and look, but I was afraid, for multiple reasons. I was afraid I'd see Aton and his cronies trying to stop us from escaping. I was also afraid of seeing what happened to me and my body when I travelled by faerie.

Instead I grasped Blackthorne's hands tighter and leaned my head down to meet Lily's. I could hear Lily chanting quietly, lending what little support she could to her fellow faerie.

We tipped to one side, sliding off-balance and I panicked, afraid I would fall. "You'll be ok," Lily called to me. "Just hold on tight and keep your eyes shut, Hero."

That made me feel better about my decision not to open my eyes before. Apparently Lily didn't think I'd like what I saw either. I pulled myself as close to my faerie partners as I could and began my own chant. "Please, God, let us be safe. Please. God, let us be safe." I mumbled over and over again under my breath.

Soon the voices were gone and the sound of the wind raged in my ears. Then, rather suddenly, it all stopped and my feet touched solid ground.

"Ok," said Blackthorne.

I opened my eyes, focusing first on Lily. She smiled at me. "We're here. We're safe, Hero." I smiled at her and forced back tears.

Letting go of Blackthorne's hands and backing away so he would have room to put Lily down gave me a moment to look around. We were in the great ante room outside of Darius' office. It was packed full of people, presumably vampires, once again.

The stoic, ever-present guard saw us and I got the most reaction I'd ever seen out of him. He turned his head back towards Darius' door and said something before zooming to us with his vampire speed.

"The Magistrate will see you now," he announced in a deep, heavily accented voice. "If you will allow me," he said as he swept Lily up in his massive arms. "Now, quickly." He said to me before taking off with the faerie.

Not being blessed, or cursed depending on your point of view, with vampire speed, I had to just settle for human speed, which I'm sure looked pretty pathetic to the on-lookers, but I didn't care. I ran as fast as my two little feet would take me. By the time I caught up with Lily, she was being laid out on one of Darius' luxurious sofas.

"Miss Fletcher, come in, come in!" Darius called to me. "My goodness! How did you manage to escape? Are you alright? Obediah, send for Dr. Galeno immediately."

"Food, drink," I blurted out desperately.

"Yes," Darius agreed with a nod. "Of course. Once you send for the doctor, arrange for something for the ladies." Obediah was gone in the blink of an eye. "Sadir!" bellowed the Magistrate. The tall, dark guard stepped into the room. So that was his name! "Get me the chest of keys."

The stoic guard zipped to some far recess of Darius' office and returned in a millisecond with a small wooden chest. He placed it next to Darius who was now kneeling beside Lily.

I had settled myself in the chair closest to Lily. It felt wonderful. It wasn't very padded or soft, but it wasn't a hard metal folding chair and it was safe. Now that I knew we were safe the adrenaline that had been spurring me on seemed to leave me. I felt limp and empty. My only concern now was that Lily be freed of her shackles.

"I'll be as gentle as I can, Miss Lacewing. Hang on." Darius reached out and took hold of the chain crisscrossed around Lily's torso. With one great tug the old Roman vampire managed to pull apart the iron chain and then he gently unwrapped it from around the weak little faerie. I was surprised at the degree of his delicacy. I would not have thought it possible. Then he opened the chest and set to work at finding a key that would open the restraints on her wrists and ankles.

There was already a slight change in Lily. The relief from the weight and the toxic touch of the iron chains showed on

130

her face and I could see, no, feel, how hard she worked to control her eagerness and anxiousness while Darius worked to free her from the shackles. Her amber eyes, so pale with weakness, nearly a thin watery yellow, were pleading with each key to be the right one.

The Magistrate, a man so feared and revered for his ruthlessness, sat at her feet patiently trying key after key; turning each one carefully. At last there was a loud click and he smiled. Darius smiled. And it wasn't one of those sarcastic vampire smiles; he was happy.

Gingerly, he pried open one side of the manacle and placed it on the sofa next to her while he worked on freeing her from the other half. Once both wrists were free, I could see how the iron had burnt her skin. Well, I guess you'd call it a burn. That's what it sort of looked like to me. Her skin was all bright red and raw looking but shiny too. Whatever it was it had done, it looked painful as hell.

Fortunately, the key also fit the lock on her ankles and she was soon completely free. Luck seemed to have decided to join our side.

At that moment, Sadir opened the door and Dr. Galeno rushed in. "I came as quickly as I could, sir. I stopped to get some extra supplies based on what Obediah told me."

"Of course," said Darius as he straightened himself up and backed away from Lily. "Please, doctor," he invited, motioning towards both Lily and myself. I wasn't sure this supernatural medicine man could help me but I was grateful that Darius was going to have him check me out just the same.

In one fluid, graceful motion, he bent himself and took up the position in front of Lily that Darius had just vacated. After a few seconds of examination he said "This is not yours?" holding the turquoise stone around her neck.

"No," said Lily quietly. "Another faerie gave that to me. My stones…" she couldn't finish. She closed her eyes tightly and tears trickled down her cheeks.

"Aton took her stones," I finished for her. "Blackthorne gave her that stone and I gave her my amethyst ring. It was all we had."

The good doctor raised an eyebrow at me, but nothing more. Darius, however raised both and shared a concerned look with Obediah, whom I had not seen return.

Dr. Galeno picked up Lily's hand and looked at the gold ring on her thumb. "This was a special gift," he stated. It was rhetorical, there was no need to tell the story now, besides, I was tired. He smiled at my friend. "Shame it wasn't in silver, but I expect it gave you some benefit just the same."

"It did, it most definitely did," answered Lily as she smiled at me.

We all waited silently while the doctor concocted his potion for Lily. When it was complete, he held it in a crystal vial and tapped it three times against the heart in the claddagh ring on Lily's thumb. The liquid went from clear to pink to a deep violet. Lily swallowed it in one gulp. It only took a few seconds to see a faint pink blush come to her cheeks. She closed her eyes and rested her head against the back of the sofa, finally beginning to feel better.

Then the doctor turned his attention to me. "Now, Miss Fletcher, let's have a look at your neck." Ugh! I so did not want anyone looking at my neck and I sure as hell didn't want anyone messing around with my neck. I wasn't sure I'd ever want anyone to ever touch my neck again.

He was very gentle as he examined the puncture wounds and the bruises. He even shook his head at them in sympathy to me and in anger at my attackers. That alone made me feel better.

After a few more minutes of poking and prodding he said "food and rest will do you the most good, but I can help you along." He fidgeted around in his medicine bag for a few minutes and then produced a vial of liquid. It was red, blood red. Needless to say I was reluctant.

However, after a quick look around the room, I realized that I would be very ungrateful not to follow the Doctor's orders. Taking a deep breath, I shot the potion down like it was tequila. Just for clarification, I don't like tequila, in fact, I hate it. It's what I imagine lighter fluid would taste like. I can't understand how anyone drinks that shit.

I am happy to report that the medicine was in no way, shape or form anything like tequila. It wasn't the tastiest thing I ever had, but it was ok. It sort of tasted like, like... I don't know. It smelled like my mother's spice rack. When I was a little girl, my mom had a spice rack that hung on the wall in the kitchen. Whenever I walked past it, I could smell all the spices mixed together. The potion smelled like that. Pungent, exotic. But it didn't taste that way. The closest thing I can think to describe it is a multivitamin.

I felt warm and tingly all over, like when you come in from a snowstorm and you shed your heavy outerwear and sit before the fireplace to warm up. My lids felt heavy and I wanted to sleep. I heard the Doctor say his goodbyes and Darius asked Obediah if there was any news of Aton.

"Holy crap!" I yelled suddenly remembering why we wanted to come and see Darius. Everyone jumped and looked at me.

"Miss Fletcher, really…" Darius began.

"I can't believe I almost forgot! Darius, I, uh, er, Magistrate, whatever! Aton is going to try and overthrow you!"

Needless to say, my announcement was followed by stunned silence. And that silence was followed by me having to explain what I'd done and how things had gotten to this point. It went about as well as you'd expect.

Pinching the bridge of his nose, eyes shut tight, Darius asked "Miss Fletcher, if I understand correctly, in order to affect your escape you tricked Aton by pretending to think his plan all along had been to overthrow me, yes?" I nodded. Yeah, his eyes were closed, but I was afraid to speak now that the truth was out.

He paced in front of his grand marble desk. "And he is now, as far as you know, speaking with Ilderim about the possibility of a coup?" I gulped and nodded again.

"Ilderim wouldn't be so foolish. He'd never go against you," offered Lily.

"I don't know that for certain. Even if he loses, he might be able to get his hands on some of the artifacts or at least access our documents. His desire for the text is as great as anyone's."

"Would he chance that even if he thought Aton would lose? Would he risk you and he being enemies just on the hope that he might be able to find something?" I asked uncertain.

Darius had stopped pacing. He stood straight and tall with his back to us. "Obediah, please show our guests to the Vienna suite. Have their meals sent to them there along with anything else they require."

We had been dismissed. I wasn't sure if he was just too angry to have us there any longer or if he wanted us out of the way so he could get down to business. Probably both.

"Take them through the back. I don't want anyone to see them," he added.

"Blackthorne is waiting for us outside," I ventured in a whisper.

Obediah turned to me and sneered. "He left before you even entered this office."

"What?" Lily and I cried in unison.

"That will be all," declared Darius without turning around.

Dutifully, Lily and I followed Obediah out of the magistrate's office via a back door hidden in the dark recesses of the large room. We passed no one in the halls and stairs as we made our way to our room. I didn't know about Lily, but I was so tired and weak, the only thing that kept me going was the idea that food was being sent to this room for me and that the last thing I needed in a mansion full of vampires was to be found lying unconscious somewhere.

At last we reached our destination and Obediah grudgingly showed us in. "What's your problem?" I barked, unable to restrain myself.

Obediah looked at me like a bug he wanted to squash. "You put my master in danger."

"Actually, all you guys put me in danger getting me mixed up in this crap in the first place. If it wasn't for vampires I wouldn't have had been put in a position to make up a story like that to save my skin!"

"Hero!" Lily cautioned uselessly.

Obediah just sneered at me and said "Your food should be here momentarily. Please don't leave the room unless you are sent for."

"Hang on." Yes, that was me. Like you had to ask? "What if we need something? How do we get in touch with you, or…. someone else?"

He sniffed impatiently. "A guard will be posted here shortly. You can let him know if you require anything." And with that, he was gone. I was really going to miss him.

"Ugh!" I groaned after he left. "I can't stand him!"

"I know he's a real pill, but you shouldn't antagonize him, Hero."

"I wouldn't be me if I didn't." With that, I flopped myself down on the enormous bed. It was perhaps the biggest bed I'd ever seen, but I was too worn out to appreciate it. Only the pathetic grumble of my long empty stomach kept me from falling fast asleep. It knew that food was on its way and wasn't giving up no matter how soft and comfy the bed was.

"I can't believe Blackthorne bailed on us. Where do you think he went?"

"I don't know," replied Lily as she came around the other side of the bed and climbed in. "He couldn't go back and he couldn't go home. He was safe here. I'm too tired to think why he left or where he's gone." She curled up in a ball and went right out.

Her color was getting slowly better. At least her skin was no longer as white as her hair. The skin around her wrists and ankles was still bright red and looked horrendously sore. I couldn't tell if it had healed at all, but if it had, it wasn't much. Was this due in part to Lily being without her own stones? I looked at my claddagh ring shining on her thumb. I was glad it was of some help to her. I didn't know what kind or how much, but the knowledge that it did her any good, no matter how small was a comfort to me.

There was a squeaky-squealing noise out in the hallway followed by some muffled voices. Food! I sat up and leapt off the bed with more energy that I would have thought possible as our guard opened the door and allowed a cart full of delicious smelling food to be wheeled in.

Oh! I could have cried! Food! Thank you, God! Real food! I couldn't wait for the guy to set everything up all nice and hoity-toity. I started lifting covers. Beef Wellington, Chicken Piccata, Baked-Stuffed Shrimp, herb-roasted potatoes, green beans almandine, glazed carrots, garden salad and an entire chocolate cake!

"Thank you, oh, thank you!" I blubbered as I pulled up a chair.

"What can I serve you, madam?" asked the server.

"Uh, just pour me something to drink and leave everything else, please. I'll serve myself. Thank you."

He didn't seem thrilled with that idea but he wasn't going to argue. After pouring me a glass of iced water with lemon and a glass of red wine of some kind he asked if I needed anything else. "No, I don't think so. Thank you very much. It's all wonderful!"

Once he left I dug in with abandon. To my shock and horror I thought at first I might be ill and unable to hold the food down after going without for a few days. Thankfully, I think it was more just my terribly frazzled nerves that balked at the first few bites of food.

It all tasted so good. I wanted to cry. You probably think that's silly, but it's true. I was so happy to have food again and that it was excellent food, expertly prepared. It wasn't like my first food after my ordeal was a McDonald's hamburger or a bag of Dorito's. Don't get me wrong, I wouldn't have turned up my nose at either. But the fact that I had this huge table of beautifully cooked and presented food and could eat to my heart's and stomach's content after what I'd been through, well, I'm sorry, in the words of Leslie Gore, 'you would cry too if it happened to you.'

Before you ask, no, I didn't eat the entire chocolate cake. I didn't even eat half. In fact I only had one slice. By the time I made my way to the cake I was already pretty full. I know, you're shocked that I didn't just dive right into the cake first and forego the real food, but aside from it all smelling and looking so good, I knew my body needed that more than my psyche needed the chocolate. Don't be shocked. Even in my weakened condition I was perfectly capable of knowing what was best for me. You just assume I always make bad decision. Tsk, tsk, tsk. So not fair! Besides, you know what they say about assuming.

When I couldn't even look at another bite of food, yes, that includes the chocolate, I wiped my mouth on the linen napkin and stumbled over to the bed. I climbed in carefully so as not to disturb Lily who was still asleep.

My limbs felt heavy and for the first time in days I believed I would be ok. It only took seconds for me to fall fast asleep.

Chapter 11

Bacon. Mmm. Oh yeah, I love bacon. Where was that coming from? Everything was dark but I could smell bacon. Crisp, delicious fried pork!

Slowly my eyes opened and I realized I had not been dreaming. I saw Lily seated where I had been some hours before but now the table was laden with breakfast foods. Pancakes, thick French toast, scrambled eggs, fresh fruit, sausages and, of course, bacon.

"Holy crap that smells good!" I declared as I climbed out of the bed.

"It is. There's plenty, come and get it!"

Silly girl! I was already sitting at the table before she could finish her sentence and reaching to fill my plate.

I was glad to see Lily eating. She looked wonderful. Her complexion was back to normal and the skin on her wrists, while still red and sore looking, were greatly improved since last I looked.

"How are you feeling?" I asked.

"Mmm." She nodded. "Much better, thank you. How are you, Hero?"

"A lot better. So much!" I said as I munched a bite of bacon. It was even better than it had smelled.

"Do you have any idea what time it is?" I asked out of curiosity.

"I think it's around nine or nine-thirty."

"In the morning, I assume?"

She nodded and gestured toward the table full of breakfast food.

"Yeah, well. I just wanted to be sure. For all I knew you requested this." We both laughed. It felt good to laugh.

I remembered when I had last laughed and it had the opposite effect on me. "Lily," I asked somberly. "I've been afraid to ask. Hazel, is she ok?"

"Yes," she answered, slightly surprised. "Why have you been afraid to ask?"

"I was afraid Aton's men might have done something to her when they took me."

"Oh, I see. I'm sorry, Hero. I didn't even think to tell you. When Hazel saw you being taken she went to the head of our tribe. They didn't have a chance to get to her. She's safe."

It was a great relief and I felt my shoulders relax and sag with the revelation. There were others on my mind though. "What about Jaeger, have you heard anything about him?"

Lily blinked at me. I know she found it odd that I would ask about him. "I've heard no news about Jaeger at all. Why?"

I didn't like that. "He was supposed to be watching me; looking out for me. I don't know how they got past him."

Lily had no response but I could tell she didn't like the idea of Aton and his men getting around Jaeger any more than I did.

"What about Kin? Have you heard anything about him?"

"Should I have?" she asked confused.

"No," I replied, trying not to sound too dejected. "He's away on business for Darius and I," I paused to sigh. "I didn't know if he might be on his way home yet."

My little faerie friend reached across the snow-white table cloth and squeezed my hand. "I'm sure he'll be back as soon as he can."

"Thanks," I said with a smile I didn't really feel. I didn't want to talk any more so I dedicated myself to consuming French toast and bacon and sausage with far too much maple syrup.

Once we had both had our fill we pushed away from the table and went to sit in the living area of the suite. "Do you think there's any chance I could ask for clean clothes?" I wondered as I looked down at three tiny spots of syrup on my shirt.

"Sure, why not?"

"Well, food is one thing, I don't expect Darius to have women's clothing at hand for someone who might need it."

"If he doesn't have what you need, he'll send someone for it."

"Seriously?" She nodded emphatically. "Wow. So... if I make a request for a change of clothes, do you want some too?"

It was agreed. We both wanted to shower or bathe and get into clean clothes. Lily found a pen and paper inside a desk drawer and began to list what we would need. I told her what size I needed for pants, shirt and underclothes. I wasn't too happy about that part, but there wasn't much point in getting all clean just to put dirty skivvies back on, and I don't do commando.

Lily went to the door and gave a little rap on it before she opened it slightly. She said a few quiet words to the guard and handed him the list. He didn't seem to think there was anything at all strange with the request. I took that as a good sign.

"What do you think is happening?" I asked after she came back to the sofa.

"Happening?"

143

"With Aton and Ilderim and the whole thing. Do you really think Aton will be stupid enough to try and take out Darius?"

"I don't know. I really know nothing about Aton and don't know enough about Ilderim and his ambitions to guess whether he'd risk making such an enemy."

"You know about this text thingy though, right? The one Darius mentioned that Ilderim might want to get more info on badly enough that he might take the chance."

"Yes, the faeries are aware of it. We have no interest in the book. It holds nothing for us or our kind."

"What do you mean?"

She shrugged her shoulders. "Its contents have no bearing on the faeries and our brother and sister creatures."

"What kind of creatures does it have a bearing on? Vampires and shifters obviously, but who else?"

"Kin has not told you about it?"

"Not very much." Ok, a cryptic reply, I grant you, but I wanted to know what the damn thing was.

Lily hesitated to continue. "Please," I begged. "Tell me what you know about it. My life has been put in danger because of the stupid thing already and who the hell knows what else might happen. I just want to understand why it's so important."

She spent a long, awkward silence looking at the tender skin around her wrists; weighing the pros and cons. At long last she said, "I cannot tell you all I know, Hero. There are some things I am forbidden to speak of, even if I wanted to. But I will tell you what I can."

"Thank you, Lily. I really appreciate it. What is this thing? What is it called?"

She shook her head slowly. "No, I do not think I should tell you its name. The vampires never use it. If you should ever speak it accidentally they will know someone has told you about it. Besides, knowing its name will not alter anything. The text is a large manuscript. No one knows exactly how old it is. It is rumored to have been written by several people, vampire and shifter as well as human. It is most likely a collaborative or collective work. Its pages are said to contain spells and incantations to increase power, dominate others and destroy enemies. But the most important secret it's whispered to hold is the spell to reverse the Curses of the Damned."

"Curses of the Damned?" That sounded big. Ok, it sounded like something from Indiana Jones or Scooby Doo, but it still sounded important.

Lily took a deep breath. "Yes. Those that are thought to be victims of curses of eternal damnation - vampires, shifters, werewolves, mummies, zombies etc. Any once-human or part-human being who is cursed with a supernatural existence."

"I, I don't understand. Don't supernatural beings think they are superior to humans? They wouldn't want to be just human again." I looked curiously at Lily. "Would they?"

"There are those that would. There are those that would use the text to rid the world of particular species and preserve only their own."

"So the spell doesn't just reverse the curse for all of them, it's individual to each kind of supernatural being?"

"Yes, that's right."

I had visions of red, white and blue 'Reverse the Curse' banners and signs in my head. So much worse than anything the Great Bambino ever did. Though I have to admit there are some Sox fans that would probably argue the case.

Werewolves, mummies, zombies, etc. I was glad she stopped at 'etc.' and didn't expand her list. Zombies were real? I knew a lot of gamers and movie makers that would be thrilled to hear that, not to mention a few reality show producers.

"And the faeries aren't concerned with the text because? Because you guys aren't cursed. You're born magical, right?"

She smiled at me. "Something like that, yes."

"But aren't you concerned about it falling into the wrong hands?"

"It's been lost for hundreds of years. We're not going to worry about something that might never be found."

"So, what happens if somebody finds this book and uses one of those reverse curses?"

"Well, depending on which spell they use and their power, they could potentially lift the curse off of hundreds of thousands of their kind."

"If someone like Darius were to find it, how many vampires do you think he could free?"

"North America," she answered without missing a beat.

I drew back in surprise at both the scope and quickness of her answer. "Wow," I breathed as I tried to wrap my head around the implications.

"Wait a minute. You said there were spells to reverse the Curses of the Damned."

"Yes," Lily answered.

"Does it contain the actual Curses of the Damned?"

Lily hesitated. "I, uh, I'm not sure. I would expect so."

"So, if Darius could un-curse the whole of North America, he could also *curse* all of North America and make them into an enormous vampire army?"

"No! No, no." Lily stammered. "He wouldn't do that, no one would do that."

"You don't think so? Leontine would gladly have rid the world of humans and turned them all into shifters."

Lily's eyes darted back and forth as her brain worked furiously to make sense of the scenario I had presented. "No, it would be insanity to do something like that. Who would vampires feed off of if the entire continent were vampires?"

"Ok, good point. But shifters eat regular food, don't they? What about werewolves and the, uh, others?"

She just kept shaking her head and saying 'no' over and over. My suggestion had unnerved her. It hadn't done me a lot of good either.

We sat in uncomfortable silence, each contemplating horrific outcomes if the text were ever to be found. Each was too awful to utter out loud.

A sharp knock on the door startled us and shook us out of our dark thoughts. I went to the door and said "Yes?" Ok, sure, there was a guard at the door so I could have just opened it, but you can't really blame me for being cautious can you?

"Your clothing," a gravelly voice barked simply. I opened the door and the guard passed through two white shopping bags.

"Thank you," I said before closing the door. I took the bags back to the sofa so I could examine their contents with Lily.

It was pretty obvious whose was whose. Lily was so very tiny. I wasn't heavy by any means, but I was taller and not nearly so narrow and thin as the little faerie.

I pulled out a standard pair of jeans and a generic pale blue button down blouse. Not fabulous but at least they were clean. The bag also contained undergarments, socks and sneakers. Where these items came from so quickly, I had no idea and frankly, I didn't want to think about it. All that mattered was that they were clean and that the undergarments still had tags on them.

"Why don't you go ahead and shower first," I suggested to Lily. I was aware that faeries were more aware of odors and scents than humans and I'm sure she still could detect traces of the iron that had bound her.

"Thank you, Hero. I won't be long, I promise."

"Take as long as you need. It's not like we have anywhere to go." Which was true. Just what the heck were we supposed to do all day?

While Lily showered I thought some more about the stupid text thing. Part of me was sorry I'd asked. What did Darius plan to do with the thing if and when he found it? Just how close was he to finding it? Did he know exactly how many artifacts there were left to be found and if so, did he know where they were?

Ugh! Too many questions. Correction, too many dramatic questions. My mind felt like the ending of an old movie serial with some death-defying cliffhanger dangling before the frantic, awe-struck audience. But this wasn't the movies. There was no Superman or Zorro or Dick Tracy to come and save the day in the opening of the next episode.

True to her word, Lily was quickly out of the shower and looking much happier for it. The heather-gray t-shirt and black leggings were a bit loose on her though I suspected that like me she could care less as long as they were clean.

"All yours!" she chirped brightly.

"Thanks," I said as I walked past her with the bundle of new clothes under my arm. I hoped the shower would do as much for my disposition as it had for hers.

The hot water felt wonderful. I marveled that Lily was able to force herself out from under the spray so quickly. I unwrapped a tiny bar of lavender soap and the aroma instantly filled my senses. I had to wonder if there had been some magical ingredient or charm placed on the soap the way it soothed my nerves, relaxed my muscles and eased the ache in my temples. The scent made me think of sunny fields and green grass and pale purple blossoms. It was heavenly.

I lingered in the shower as long as I dared. Lily had been so quick and thoughtful and I didn't want to appear selfish and rude.

It was weird but still good to put on the new clothes. They weren't mine nor were they something I would buy but they were clean and bore no memories of the horrors of the past few days.

The bathroom was full of all necessary toiletries and grooming needs. I ran a large, wide-toothed comb through my towel-dried hair and powdered the bruises on my poor abused neck.

Deciding that was as good as I was going to get and that I didn't feel like bothering with the hair dryer, I padded out into the suite in my stocking feet. Silly phrase isn't it?

"Feel better?" Lily asked.

"I do," I replied. "What are the odds it's going to last?" I added in my usual sarcastic manner and we both laughed.

"I don't know, but I'll take it while I can get it."

"I'm glad to see you're feeling so much better," I told her. "I was so worried about you." She wiggled her thumb at me and smiled. "Ok, what am I missing about the ring?"

"Amethyst is an important stone. It heals psychically as well as mentally. It brings inner peace and strength, something I desperately needed to get me through yesterday. Normally, a stone that wasn't my own would have barely any impact, but you gave me this stone out of a pure desire to help me even though it has special meaning to you. That makes a big difference. The gift itself creates a powerful magic." Her eyes were glassy, on the verge of tears.

"You knew it had been given to me," I recalled out loud.

"Mmm. I can feel the love that flows through this piece," she said as she ran her fingertip over the purple heart.

I have to be completely honest here. I was conflicted at this moment. While I felt just awful about Lily having her stones taken and I felt responsible for it (though that spineless Blackthorne was responsible too), I was sad at the thought of never having my claddagh ring again. Lily was right, it was something very special to me, but I could hardly begrudge her having it after all that had happened. I knew it was enormously difficult for a faerie to bond with new stones if she lost her own.

I took her hand in mine and squeezed it gently. I wanted to tell her that I was happy that I was able to give her any comfort at all after what she had been through but all I could do was look at her lovely amber eyes and smile. I felt the tears well up in my eyes. Damn! I didn't want to get all mushy!

She squeezed back and smiled and we both laughed to keep from getting too sentimental. It had been a nice moment but we needed to lighten the mood.

"So!" I said, "What shall we do to pass the time? Play cards? Charades? Annoy the guard?"

"Actually, I want to call someone."

Oh! Hadn't seen that coming. I wondered if Lily had a sweetheart. "Sure," I said.

"I want to let the head of my tribe know about Blackthorne and what's going on with Darius."

That made sense. I hadn't thought about Lily's tribe being able to come and assist Darius. I wonder if he'd already contacted them himself and said so to Lily.

"Oh, I doubt that. Shannon is difficult to track down."

"Shannon?"

"She's the head of our tribe. She stays pretty well out of sight. Being the head of a faerie tribe is pretty dangerous so you have to take a lot of precautions."

"Why is it so dangerous?"

"Well, you have to be born to rule a tribe. It's like a royal bloodline. And there are only so many tribes and faeries live for hundreds of years."

"So Shannon should know a lot about avoiding a hostile takeover?" I finished for her.

"You could say that," she replied with a smile.

Chapter 12

Our guard was skeptical at our request for a phone and said he'd have to get approval from Darius. That was fine with us. We had all the time in the world.

"Is there anything Shannon can do to get your stones back? Any kind of spell or something?"

Lily shook her head sadly.

"Oh. Sorry. I was hoping there was some sort of homing spell or something she could do to bring them back where they belong."

The faerie grinned half-heartedly. "It's a nice idea but I know of no such spell."

"What will she do about Blackthorne? Will she be able to save his sister?"

She sighed. "I don't know. To be honest, I don't even know if he and Mari are still alive after he helped us to escape."

I hadn't thought about that. Well, I hadn't wanted to think about that. I admit it, I didn't like Blackthorne. I think we've already covered this. I didn't know his sister and I certainly didn't want anything to happen to her, especially on account of me, but given a choice between me getting killed or a stranger getting killed, I'm going to have to go with the stranger. Ok, perhaps no the Christian attitude, I grant you, but there it is.

"Is, is she your friend, this Mari?"

Lily nodded. "We're not close like Hazel and I are, but she's my friend."

"I'm sorry," I whispered.

"No need for you to be sorry, Hero. Blackthorne should never have left the tribe, even if he was in love. It's not safe for us to separate."

"Obviously." Damn. Couldn't help myself. It was out of my mouth before I knew what I was doing. I smiled sheepishly and she smiled back. Thank goodness Lily 'got me'.

A little while later our phone arrived. The guard came in and plugged in a cordless phone base into a jack by the desk, checked to be sure the handset worked and then marched out without a word. It must be some vampire security requirement to only speak when absolutely necessary.

"Some might like him for his swarthy good looks, but it's his fascinating gift of conversation that won me over," I joked as Lily went to retrieve the phone.

She laughed at me over her shoulder. 'Don't deny it, you are crazy for his little goatee!"

"Oh! Yeah, that's it!" I quipped as I rolled my eyes.

Lily sat down and rapidly dialed a series of numbers. After a few seconds she spoke to someone in another language. It sounded like it was probably Celtic, but I wasn't sure. For all I knew it was Welsh or something.

She spoke quickly and quietly, her manner intent and alert. The joking air of a mere few seconds ago was gone and forgotten.

"Aye!" she said sharply and pressed the receiver down hard. Then she let it up and began dialing furiously again. Another conversation in a foreign tongue ensued, just as determined as the last.

After a few more calls, none of which I understood except for a few 'ayes' and a couple of 'nos' and my name once or twice, Lily got up from the desk and came back over to me.

"Well, that's that." She seemed sad again.

"What is it? Have they had news?" I was afraid her friend had been killed.

"No," she said shaking her head. "They knew nothing of what was going on. One of the pitfalls of faerie life. We like to live where our neighbors can't really see us, for obvious reasons. So, when someone like me is taken, if no one is expecting to see me, they don't know I'm missing."

I gasped a little. "You mean no one knew you'd been taken?!"

She shook her head. "Nope. And Blackthorne had never told them about being blackmailed to reveal Hazel's information."

"Well, I can't say I'm surprised."

"But we could have helped protect him and his loved ones if he had told us. Instead he kept quiet and fell victim again." She was angry now. That was a good sign; it meant she was getting better. That was the Lily I knew. Get pissed at stupidity and weakness.

"Were you able to reach Shannon?"

"Aye," she said out of habit. "She is on her way to meet with Darius. She should be here any time now."

I wondered if I'd get to meet her.

"Hazel?"

"She's fine. Relieved to hear you're alive, of course."

I felt bad that my friend had been so worried about me but glad to confirm that she was safe. Not that I had doubted Lily, but considering the events of the past few days it was nice to have some definite good news.

"What will Shannon do? Or is there anything she can do?" I was unsure that the leader of the faerie tribe would get involved more than necessary.

"I really don't know," Lily responded after a pause. "Darius has been fair and decent to our tribe. That's not as common as you might think among vampires and faeries."

I shrugged. "Honestly, Lily, I can't say I ever thought about it."

"No," she said with a smile, "I don't suppose you would have at that. Some vampires feel that despite our magic that we are weak little creatures that should be dominated and our magic exploited. There are places in this world where faeries are hunted by vampires to be made slaves."

"Sort of like Blackthorne?"

"Oh, no. Blackthorne was foolish and was taken advantage of because of what he knew and it's a pity, I'll grant that. But it's not the same as these poor souls that are imprisoned and tortured for the sake of their magic."

She shivered and I reached out and took her hand. "I'm sorry. It must be awful to know your fellow faeries are treated like that."

Lily dipped her head sadly. "Yes," she said quietly.

After a long pause I asked "So do you think Shannon will stand by Darius if it comes to it?"

"Probably. I can't see someone like Aton treating our tribe well. We try to avoid vampire politics but it's in our best interest to keep Darius in charge."

I wanted to ask how the faeries would help. Would they fight? Could they cast protective spells or spells to increase success in battle? But it was pretty obvious that Lily didn't want to discuss the topic further. We sat quietly, holding hands, each wondering and worrying what the next few hours would bring.

The Vienna suite may have been beautiful and luxurious but it was awfully dull, even when sharing it with a faerie. There was no television or any kind of entertainment or distraction. When I pulled back the heavy curtains to look out the one window I found it was cloaked with a metal security blind on the outside. Lovely!

I thought of asking the security guard for a deck of cards but I didn't think he'd appreciate such a trivial request. So I entertained myself by imagining requesting all sorts of silly and ridiculous things and what his reaction might be. How would he react if I asked him to get me some nail polish so I could paint my toenails? What if I told him I needed music and told him to get me some Slim Whitman and Wayne Newton albums? I could always send him for a Dunkin Donuts Coffee Coolatta. Maybe a Dairy Queen Blizzard with a bunch of complicated ingredients? I'd love to see his face if I asked for some tampons? Would he even know what I was talking about?

Oh damn, why'd I have to go and think about a Blizzard? Now I actually wanted one. Was it lunchtime yet? I looked at the clock on the mantle. Close enough. By the time it got here it would be.

"What would you like for lunch?" I asked my roommate.

"Lunch? Is it lunchtime already?" When I assured her it was near enough she replied "Oh, anything I guess. Some fruit would be nice."

I went to the door and knocked. The surly guard promptly opened the door and furrowed his brows at me. "I'd like to order lunch, please."

"I'll tell them to send something up," he said shortly.

"Wait!" I called before he could close the door. "I want to request something in particular for lunch." He was less than thrilled. "We would like fresh fruit salad, Caesar chicken wraps, well-done French fries and fresh baked rolls. And afterward I'd like some Ben and Jerry's New York Super Fudge Chunk sent up. That's a type of ice cream. Two half-pints." Not that I planned on eating two half-pints. I just wasn't planning on sharing mine and wanted to make sure there was some for Lily.

"Anything else?" he asked with a sneer.

"Yes, actually. Now that you mention it. I'd like some nail polish remover, cotton balls and a new bottle of Revlon nail polish in Facets of Fuchsia." I couldn't help myself.

He gaped at me for a moment and then closed the door. I suppose he was afraid to ask if there was anything else.

"Did you just ask him for nail polish?" Lily marveled as I walked back to the sofa.

"Mmm hmm."

"What on earth for?"

"Because I'm bored, he annoyed me and it will give me something to do after lunch."

Lily laughed at me. "You are too much, Hero."

Lunch arrived much quicker than I would have expected given that I specially requested everything but I wasn't about to complain. As usual, it was all delicious. I could get used to eating here, as long as I didn't have to stay here of course.

Just as we finished our sandwiches another tray arrived. There were two crystal bowls heaping with ice cream and a chilled, insulated dish containing enough for second helpings. They even added bowls of hot fudge, whipped cream, chopped nuts and cherries so we could make sundaes. And off to one side was lovely ceramic box with nail polish remover, cotton pads and the exact nail polish I had requested. A girl could get spoiled here.

"Cool," I said as I admired my sparkly purple toenails some time later. I wiggled them and watched as the light twinkled off of the glittery nail enamel.

I offered the polish to Lily but she passed, though she did say she admired the way my toenails looked.

"Ughh!" I groaned when the novelty of my painted toes wore off. "I am so sick of this room! I want to know what's going on!"

"Me too," agreed Lily. "Waiting around isn't my thing."

"Alright then!" I marched to the door and wrapped hard. I'm sure the guard was less than pleased, but he was about to be even less than less than pleased. Ok, that sounded better in my head.

"We want to see Darius." I think he would have much preferred I ask for more nail polish. While I waited for him to pick his chin up off the floor I pressed on. "Please get word to him that we would like to see him."

"Bu-but you can't just,"

"Well if we can't, let Darius be the one to say so," Lily interjected as she joined me by my side.

The befuddled guard just looked from one of us to the other, desperately hoping to see some sign that this was a joke or that we would withdraw our request. Wasn't going to happen.

"Go on," I told him as I shooed him away with my hands. I admit I got a twisted sense of pleasure from that little gesture.

He closed the door and Lily and I held our breath for a moment before we burst into giggles. You're probably thinking 'it wasn't that funny' but when you've spent a few days waiting to be killed your humor threshold is significantly lowered. Plus, screwing with vampires is fun.

And so we went back to waiting.

After what seemed like an eternity, but was probably more like twenty minutes, the door opened and in walked Darius, unannounced. We awkwardly jumped to our feet.

"Darius! Oh crap! I mean Magistrate!" I fumbled.

Darius just closed his eyes and shook his head almost imperceptibly. "You two required to see me?"

"We're going stir crazy in here not knowing wh-"

"Am I to understand you called me here because you are *bored*?" he accused, his voice rising with each syllable. He was back to being the scary, I-wouldn't-want-to-run-into-him-in-a-dark-alley Darius. Gone was the caring and considerate Darius of yesterday.

Lily quickly jumped in. "Forgive us Magistrate. A poor choice of words. Won't you please sit?" She gestured to a chair opposite the sofa where we had been sitting. Darius looked back and forth between us, uncertain there was any reason to keep him here. "We do have something to discuss, truly."

Deciding that Lily would not dare deceive him, Darius sat down. "Now that we have had time to recover and are feeling more ourselves, we are anxious to see if there is anything else we might recall that would be of help to you or if we may be useful in any other way."

"And," I began, grinding to a halt when both heads snapped around to stare at me. I cleared my throat. "And I was hoping you might tell me how Jaeger is doing?"

That took Darius off guard. "Jaeger? Why would you inquire after him?"

"Because he was looking out for me when I was taken. They had to have done something to him in order to get to me. I've, well, I've been concerned about him."

Darius stared at me quizzically. "I forget the human tendency to waste emotion on such trivial things."

I'm sure you can imagine all the lovely retorts that sprang to mind. Oh, how I longed to tell him what trivial things I was thinking about him at the moment.

"I'm sorry you feel that my concerns are a trivial waste, but if anything happened to him it would be because of me and I'd feel responsible."

He shook his head sadly and looked at me like a child unable to comprehend the simplest of concepts. "My dear Miss Fletcher, Jaeger was unharmed, but had he been harmed it would not have been because of you but rather because he was performing his duties as assigned to him by his Magistrate."

'Well, the hell with you then,' was on the tip of my tongue and, oh boy, did I want to spit that out at him, but, I held it in. Bet you didn't think I could, did you?

I bit the inside of my cheek and said "Thank you for letting me know he's ok."

"If there is nothing else," Darius said as he stood.

In for a penny, in for a pound. "Yes, have you heard from Kin?"

This time when both heads snapped around there was no surprise on their faces. There was a look of 'you've got to be kidding me' on Darius' face and 'what the hell's the matter with you?' on Lily's.

Darius began walking to the door. I wasn't sure if he was going to answer me. "Kinley will be here shortly. He's on his way from the airport. And before you ask, Miss Fletcher, no, he does not know anything about what has transpired. Now if you ladies will excuse me, I have some rather important matters to attend to."

He sailed out the door without so much as a look over his shoulder. "What an ass!" I exclaimed.

"Hero! He'll hear you!" cried Lily.

"So what? We told him we might be helpful, that we might have remembered info that could be helpful and he didn't so much as ask us a single question. And all that crap about Jaeger. Can't he just be magnanimous and tell me that Jaeger is ok and thank you?"

"Well, he's got a lot on his mind."

"Oh, please! He didn't even mention Shannon to you."

"There's no reason he should have, Hero. I'm not a tribal elder or anything. Darius isn't going to share information with us."

"Then why did you support me in asking to talk to him?"

"Because I wanted him to know that we were ready and able to be of use to him."

"We didn't have to tell him that face to face."

"We did. He needed to see that we were healed and not afraid to face a difficult task."

"And seeing him was a difficult task? Seriously?" She nodded. "You supernatural types have a very strange way of doing things."

At least Kin was on his way and I would see him soon. And it was a relief to know that Jaeger was ok, even if I still had no idea how they got around him.

Suddenly, a strange voice echoed from the bathroom. "Is he gone?" I yelped and jumped a mile.

A small framed woman with long dark hair stepped out of the bathroom. She went straight to Lily and embraced her. They exchanged a few words in another language. This must be Shannon.

"And you must be Hero," she said as if reading my mind. The little faerie came and hugged me. "Thank you so much for saving our sister."

"It's ok," I said stupidly, feeling like a fraud because it was my fault she was taken to begin with.

"It's more than ok, we are grateful! I have a gift for you from our tribe. Hazel picked it out." She held up a silver chain with a pendant. It had three bright blue stones set in a triangular shape.

"Oh, it's lovely! What kind of stone is that?"

"It's three different stones actually. Tourmaline, aquamarine and blue topaz. Each stone has different qualities that Hazel felt would be beneficial to you. The setting is the Celtic Triskele which has great meaning to us." Shannon placed the necklace around my neck. Maybe it was the power of suggestion, but I felt a wonderful sense of peace flow through me.

"Thank you, thank you very much. I'll treasure it."

I was overwhelmed. I could tell by the expressions on Lily and Shannon's faces that a gift from the tribe was no small thing. This was major to them. "I wish I had something better to say," I laughed uncomfortably. "I feel like 'thank you' is so inadequate."

"No, no," replied Shannon. "That necklace is our thanks to you. If not for you, who knows what may have happened to her."

I couldn't take it. "But it's my fault she was taken in the first place."

"What?" the cried in unison.

I told them about my idea for escape that had led to Aton taking Lily prisoner. "Oh no, Hero. Aton did not take Lily because of you. It was Blackthorne's doing."

"But all Blackthorne did was tell them where to find her," I protested.

Shannon shook her head. "I'm afraid he did more than that. Aton wanted the name of a faerie with access to a lot of tribal information but whose presence would not be missed right away."

"He knew it wasn't unusual for me to be out of touch for days at a time so that made me a good target," Lily added.

I suppose that made sense. Now that I thought about it, the only reason I could come up with that Aton picked Lily to abduct was because she was my friend. Not particularly strategic now that I thought about it.

"Is there any news about his sister?" I asked, changing the subject.

"No. We haven't located her yet." The tribal leader became quiet.

"What about Blackthorne? What will happen to him?"

The faeries exchanged looks. "I think for now we will have to wait and see," replied Shannon cryptically.

"I have to go now," she announced. "Darius does not know I was coming to see you. I need to go back and address the tribe."

"Will you be fighting with Darius?" I asked.

Shannon looked at me and smiled. "I see what Darius means about you." She kissed Lily on the cheek and disappeared.

"So…," I said to Lily. "Now we wait, again."

"Mmm." She agreed. "And plan."

"Plan?" My interest was piqued. "What are we planning?"

"Among other things, how to defend ourselves when the battle starts."

Chapter 13

I'm sure you're all wondering what's been going on outside the Vienna suite while Lily and I have been recuperating.

You'd no doubt love a 'meanwhile, back in Darius' office' or 'in the meantime, Aton was busy…' Well, guess what? I'd love to give you one. Hell! I'd love someone to give me one! I'm sick to death of these four pastel papered walls and the ugly guard outside the door.

I may be clever, sharp-witted and cute, but I'm not omnipotent.

"Hey, Lily, this necklace that your tribe gave me, it doesn't have any kind of magic does it?"

She raised her eyebrows. "No. Just the natural properties of the stones. Why?"

"I just wanted to make sure I didn't find out after the battle is over that all I had to do was click my heels together three times and say 'there's no place like home'."

Her brows rose even higher. "Ok, I know you're not human, but you live in our world. Surely you've seen the 'Wizard of Oz'?"

"Oh. That sounds familiar. I probably saw it once."

Since my gape got no response, I picked up my chin and moved on. "So what can we do to protect ourselves here? And why can't we leave the room anyway?"

"No doubt Darius doesn't want them to know we are here."

"What? Oh come on! We made quite an entrance in the waiting room. It'd be kind of hard to pretend we weren't here."

"True, but Darius could get to those vampires and ensure they keep quiet. In fact I'd be surprised if he let anyone in or out of the mansion after we arrived."

I hadn't thought of that. "But a faerie could just pop out, or whatever."

She smiled at me. "Darius does not keep faeries on his staff. We are only here when sent for or when Shannon sends us on a commission."

"Do you think anyone who was here would dare betray Darius?"

"I don't know. It would be unlikely, but I just don't know."

"So why would he really have to worry about us being seen?"

There was no answer for that. I didn't know if we'd ever get one either.

"So, we just sit here and wait for the battle to begin and to be found then? Great. We're sitting ducks."

"There has to be something we can do?"

"What? We have no magic? No powers, no anything that can beat a vampire." I kicked over the chair Darius had been sitting in in frustration.

"Unless," I said turning to Lily with a grin. "We could arm ourselves with some stakes?" That was the end of life for that chair.

We ransacked the room, breaking up any piece of furniture or decoration that could be fashioned into stakes. Fortunately, the lunch dishes had not been carted away. Even though they were unnecessary, the place settings had contained knives. They came in handy carving the broken legs and supports into points.

I flashed back on *The Lost Boys* and Corey's running around town getting holy water, buying garlic and making stakes. I couldn't help smiling and recalling my favorite line. "I'll pray I never need to call ya." Great movie. I'd have to ask Kin if he'd seen it. He had a love/hate relationship with vampire movies, as I'm sure you could understand.

Kin. He'd be here soon! Thank goodness this time I wouldn't have to go through this alone! Well, not that I was alone, I had Lily, but I meant that I'd have a vampire there on my side. Ugh. The damsel in distress thing rearing its ugly head again.

Yes, that's still an issue for me. What can I say? When I have an issue, I really have it. Even after all the crap I've been through. Just add that to my list of issues.

"Well, now what?" I asked, looking around what was left of the room.

Lily shrugged. I think she felt badly about all the destruction, but I figured if a battle was going to happen here at the mansion things were going to be destroyed anyway. Besides, if a chair or a little writing desk had to give its life to save mine I wasn't going to lose sleep over it.

"I guess we should clean up," she suggested.

"No. Just the opposite. If someone does come in here after us and we hide they may think someone else has already gotten to us."

"Hmm. Maybe. It's worth a shot."

We went around and messed up the room even more. I pulled down one of the curtains, smashed the glass on some of the artwork and tossed the contents of the bed. Lily tipped over every chair and table in the room. The guard probably thought we'd gone berserk, but not enough to bother opening the door and checking.

The sudden knock on the door made me wonder if I'd been wrong about the guard's level of curiosity. To my relief and delight it wasn't the guard checking on us, it was Kin.

"Hero! My God! Thank heaven you're ok," he said as he rushed in and wrapped his arms around me.

"I'm fine, really," I assured him. It felt so good to hold him. For the first time in days I really believed things would be ok.

"If I'd had any idea of what was going…, if I knew," he tried to explain while he pressed me to his chest a little too tightly.

"It's alright, Kin. Really. I know you wouldn't have left me if you'd had even a suspicion that something was wrong. I know that."

He looked into my eyes for reassurance and nodded when he found it. "Aton," he said with his teeth clenched. "That bastard. If I get my hands on him…"

"No! He's a lunatic, Kin. You stay away from him. Let someone else worry about taking him down. He's not worth the risk."

"You think I'm afraid of him?"

Oh men! I sighed. "Of course I don't. I know you're not afraid of him. That's the whole point. You *should* be. He's insane. You going after him won't change anything that's happened or make me forget what I've gone through, so don't make things worse by risking your life unnecessarily."

174

"So you expect me to do nothing?"

"No," I said sincerely. "I expect you will do whatever it is Darius asks you to do."

We stood looking into each other's eyes for a long tense moment. It was understood: Kin was going to be put in harm's way no matter what and to his mind better to face the danger that would bring honor and satisfaction than the danger that would just fulfill a duty.

"Lily," Kin said, breaking the silence. "I'm so glad to see you looking so well. I don't know what to say."

"You don't have to say anything, Kin. I'm just so happy to know you're home and that you'll be here fighting with us."

Kin hugged her gently as though afraid she was still in pain from her shackles. As he straightened her words finally registered.

"Wait, 'with you'? You two aren't fighting."

"Why not?" I asked defiantly.

"Hero, use your head! How are you going to fight against vampires and shifters and weres? And Lily has lost her stones. How is she supposed to fight?"

"We've been making stakes," I stated proudly, and I pointed to our stash.

For the first time Kin noted the state of the room. "What happened in here?"

"We thought if we hid and it looked like someone had already been here to get us it might throw someone off."

"They'd still smell you." Leave it to Kin to spoil things.

"We've been staying here; sleeping and eating here. Even if we left, this room would smell like us, wouldn't it?" I asked.

"Yes, it would, but not as strongly as if you were actually here in the room."

"What if we hid in the bathroom and closed the door?"

"I don't know. Maybe. In the frenzy of a fight it might throw someone off, but you can't count on it working for everyone who might come in here, and then you'd be cornered in the bathroom."

Well, damn. "So what do we do then? Just sit here and wait to be killed?" Yeah, ok, not exactly constructive but I'm sure you can understand my frustration and helplessness.

"Of course not. You are well guarded, and we will all try to keep Aton and his followers from getting to you."

"But your main focus will be to keep them from getting to Darius. He must be your main concern. Not us." Lily looked Kin straight in the eye with a look that clearly communicated that she knew this to be true.

Kin nodded. He wouldn't lie, not even to try and make us feel better. "Yes, that's true. But there are a great many of us. More than there are of them and there's no reason to believe we can't keep you safe as well."

"How do you know how many are with Aton?" I asked. Seemed like a reasonable question to me.

He sighed. "I'm not entirely certain how they've come by all of their intelligence. Darius didn't have time to brief me on every detail but I know that not all of the menagerie chose to side with him. Some have come to side with Darius and some have fled, declaring their neutrality and refusal to take sides."

"Well that's cowardly."

"No it's not," said Lily. "It's actually very clever. It's a way for them to survive. They can carry on with whoever is victorious without ever having to be accused of being a traitor." I guess supernatural beings don't subscribe to the 'if you're not with me you're against me' mentality.

"So Darius has his entire clan plus some of the menagerie members and maybe the faerie tribe against Aton and whomever he could get or manipulate onto his side." I felt the need to sum everything up. Too many detective TV shows.

"Maybe the fae?" questioned Kin.

"Shannon wouldn't answer us," I explained.

"Well," interjected Lily, "she wouldn't answer you."

"What?! You mean you knew the whole time and didn't tell me?"

"You didn't ask," she said simply.

I stared at her in disbelief. "I – but you, - you heard me, I mean you knew I – " I shook my head hard. "Never mind." I couldn't let myself get upset over that now.

"We've lost track of the subject. What are Lily and I expected to do? Are we supposed to just sit here and wait to see what happens to us?"

Kin shrugged deeply and held up his hands in a clueless gesture. Not the response I was hoping for. I ran my hands through my hair and began to pace.

"Wow! Just – just – wow!" I hated the thought that I was totally helpless and just sitting here waiting for some vamp or shifter to come and kill me. True, Lily and I had some stakes and there were two of us, but how long could we defend ourselves against vampires?

Suddenly, Kin went rigid and he held up his hand to quiet me. Lily and I looked nervously from each other to Kin.

"I have to go," he announced as he embraced me one last time. "Stay here in this room Hero. Someone will be outside to protect you. You'll be fine." I kissed him and promised, but I knew he was as unsure of his declaration of safety as I was.

When he left I heard him mutter something to the guard; probably an order not to leave his post.

Once the door was shut I turned to Lily and asked "So, do we sit here and wait for them to come after us or what?"

"I vote for 'what'" she replied.

"Great! Now we just have to figure out what 'what' is."

We spent a few minutes trying to come up with ways to get past our guard, none of them very good, when another knock came upon the door. This time when the door opened a streak of red flashed through into the room.

"Hazel!" cried Lily as the two hugged each other ferociously.

"Oh, Lily! Thank the Goddess you're alright! I've been so worried about you. Oh! And you too, Hero!" she said emotionally as she reached out and pulled me into a group hug. "So very terribly worried," she sobbed.

"We're fine now Hazel, we're ok," I assured her.

"Not really though," she disagreed looking meaningfully at Lily. No, I suppose Lily wasn't really ok. She was as well as could be expected under the circumstances, but she wasn't ok.

"Here," said Hazel as she handed Lily a tiny bag of stones. "They are just travel stones, but I figured all of them combined would be enough to get you out of danger."

"I'm not going anywhere, Hazel. I intend to fight."

"I don't doubt it one bit," said the red-haired Sidhe, fighting back tears. "But there's no need to be a martyr either, dear friend. We both know too well that you, well, you are limited as to what you can contribute tonight, and if you need to get yourself to a safe distance to regroup or whatever, then these should assist you."

Very tactful, Hazel. There was no doubt the two had seen each other through many difficulties. It was sweet that Hazel had concentrated on finding a variety of the one stone that would help Lily escape the battle rather than help her fight. I felt myself getting a little choked up.

"Hazel, what's going on? Has the battle started?" I couldn't bear not knowing and I needed to change the subject before my eyes welled up.

She nodded. "On the outskirts. They haven't actually penetrated the mansion yet. We've been placing spells on the place to try and keep them out but they'll only hold so long."

"So they have other faes, not just Blackthorne, don't they?"

"Yes," acknowledged Hazel. "Not many, but then all they need are one or two powerful faes to break through."

"Why in the world would faes side with someone like Aton?"

It was Lily who answered this time. "Like I told you, faes live a very long time and there is a line of succession to be the head of a tribe. An ambitious, power-hungry fae may decide that he or she doesn't want to wait and see if they ever get their chance and instead they try and grasp whatever power they can."

Power-hungry faes teamed up with a megalomaniac vampire. Oh yay! Just what the world needed! I began to wonder if certain US politicians might not in actuality be supernatural beings. It would explain a lot.

"What can we do?" I asked, hoping against hope that Hazel might have a plan.

"I've been told to tell you to stay put," she answered sheepishly.

"Yeah, yeah. Ok, so you told us. Now what?" I may not have been friends with Hazel as long as Lily, but we knew each other well enough that she knew I wasn't going to just sit here and I knew she knew it.

Hazel looked to Lily for affirmation. "Befuddle the guard," she suggested and that was that. We were officially breaking out of the Vienna suite and joining the battle.

Chapter 14

In retrospect, I probably should have reflected a moment or two to lament our destruction in the Vienna suite but I couldn't. I have to be honest; I didn't care. I shoved a few of our hand-made stakes into my back pockets and handed a couple to Lily.

"Wait," said Hazel as we approached the door. She fished in her bag of stones and pulled out a few different stones. I couldn't see them all. One was white, one was silvery and another seemed brown or yellowish. I'm not sure if there were other stones in her hand. She stood Lily and I beside one another and began to recite words in what I assume was Celtic.

I felt myself tingling all over. I still don't know if it was Hazel's protective magic or my nerves that caused the sensation.

After a moment, Hazel returned the stones to her pouch and looked at us very solemnly. "I don't know what might happen out there. We are likely to be separated. Lily, if you need to, use those stones!" she instructed sternly. "Hero, if you must run and hide then run and hide and don't come out no matter what you hear. You'll neither of you do anyone any good dead. Better to live to fight another day, do you understand me?"

We nodded in unison. "Ok, let's go," she said.

Hazel knocked on the door and the guard opened it immediately. "Thank you," she said to him. "By the way, I should let you know," and she signaled for him to bend down so she could whisper in his ear. The guard, being anxious about the battle and as desperate for news as we were, eagerly obliged. All Hazel needed was a few precious seconds and the spell was cast.

The poor guy suddenly looked so lost and confused. He looked around as though he'd never seen that hallway before in his life.

Tapping him on the shoulder, Hazel said, "I'm glad I found you. You're wanted in the main hall."

"Oh!" he replied. Apparently he remembered the main hall. "Thank you.' And with that he strode off in the direction of the main hall.

"Ok ladies, here we go."

We tiptoed out into the hallway behind Hazel. It was eerily quiet. "Doesn't sound like a battle is raging," I whispered.

"You're going to have to trust us on that one," replied Lily. I did. Very much so.

"Lily," Hazel asked, "have you ever noticed if there are any flat areas on the roof?"

The roof! Seriously? "What?" I asked a little louder than I meant to.

"Shh!" they both reprimanded.

"I'm trying to think of the highest ground I can get to. I can cast spells over a wider area if I am on higher ground."

Oh. Ok. Having no actual knowledge of how faerie magic worked I was just going to have to trust them on this one too.

"No," answered Lily. "I think there is a small balcony on one of the back bedrooms but I think the windows are sealed off."

"Do you have some kind of spell that can open or get rid of the shutters?" I asked naively. What? Like you'd know the answer?

Hazel shook her head. "Not without destroying a large part of the room and it would take a lot of my strength to do it. It's not worth it."

Damn. "Wait a minute. Um, forgive me, but don't faeries fly? I mean, sorry if I'm wrong, I know you don't have wings or whatever, but I thought faeries could fly."

Thankfully, I didn't offend them. They smiled at me affectionately, like a parent indulging a child who asks a silly question. "We gave up our wings to live in the human realm. We couldn't exactly blend in with wings or pointed ears could we?"

Pointed ears? Wow! Never thought about that one. "Oh, well that makes sense. So, there's no way you can fly? Even with your stones?"

"Nope."

"Well, what about your travel stones? Can't you just travel from here to that balcony?"

The two fae looked at each other with wide eyes. "I suppose we could try that, but I don't know where the balcony is. I need to know where I am travelling to. That's why I drove to your house that first time, remember? When we were helping you clean up?"

I did remember. Too well. I didn't want to go down that line of thought. "So we need to get outside then. If you can see the balcony you can transport yourself to it, right?"

"I think so. Yes, I believe I could." I could see Hazel's mind whirring with the possibilities of getting onto that balcony.

"Let's find some stairs," suggested Lily and we began our journey to reach the grounds of Darius' mansion.

The irony of going down stairs to ultimately reach a location that was in the uppermost level of the mansion was not lost on me, I simply had no pithy comment to make. You're shocked I know, but sometimes sarcasm escapes even me.

I didn't like how quiet the hallway was. It seemed unnatural, even for a residence full of beings that don't need to breathe. We should have been able to hear *something*. I ached to ask Hazel and Lily if they thought the deafening silence unusual too but I didn't dare speak and be the one to disrupt the stillness.

We crept along on tiptoe, much easier for a faerie than a human, even one as little as me. I'd be jealous later. I could see the arch leading to the stairs up ahead. Unconsciously, I held my breath as we slunk the last few feet to the staircase.

Gathering at the top, we all looked down the stairwell, each expecting to see their own imagined horror screaming up towards us. Mercifully, there was nothing. Yet. Sorry, wasn't feeling 'glass half full' at that moment.

Hazel looked at us and jerked her head toward the stairs, directing us to follow her. God love her, I sure as hell wasn't going to volunteer to lead the way.

As we descended our second flight of stairs the first sounds of battle finally reached my ears. I thought my heart would explode with fear as I listened to the growling and gnashing and roars of rage. It pummeled so hard against my chest I was amazed that Hazel and Lily didn't comment on the sound.

When an especially loud scream was accompanied by the sound of, what I assume was, tearing flesh I stopped dead in my tracks. Ugh! Dead in my tracks. I really need to be more careful with my phraseology. Anyway, I stopped suddenly. I couldn't move. That sound was so incredibly awful.

"Keep moving," whispered Hazel to me as she looked back to check my progress. "Hero, come on!"

I started moving again though I felt as though I wasn't moving at all. It was like I was being moved and my body was just going along for the ride. Leave it to me of course to have a stupid, inappropriate thought at this moment. It suddenly occurred to me how valuable these sounds would be to a Hollywood sound effects artist. (Yes, I know, they are called Foley artists, but I wasn't sure if everyone knew that) My mind really thinks of the weirdest things at the weirdest times.

The lower we traveled the greater the sounds of fighting. I began to wonder at the wisdom of our plan. How would we manage to get outside? How would we manage to get anywhere at all?

Hazel stopped outside a door that was very nearly hidden, camouflaged in the natural look of the wall. I raised my eyebrows inquisitively.

"Darius," she whispered.

Oh! This must be the hidden door that Lily and I were taken through when we left his office the day we escaped from Aton. Well, that was a bit of a problem. Do we open it and risk walking into a sticky situation and pissing off Darius or do we take our chances and go below ground level and try and find another way back up to the main floor?

Both of the faeries pressed their ears to the door then shared a significant look.

"What?" I asked quietly.

"It's quiet," replied Lily. "But there may be guards stationed within the office and they might not give us the chance to explain who we are or why we are coming through this door."

Lovely! "What are our alternatives?" I didn't need to spell them out. My fae friends knew them as well as I did. Go back to the room. Stay here and hope we are well hidden. Go to another floor, either up or down, and find another staircase to take us to the main floor. Or we could take our chances with Door Number One.

"We can't just stay here." Hazel was right and we agreed. Staying there was too dangerous. If someone found us in the stairwell we'd have no chance to fight back.

"I say we try the door," I suggested. "Most of Darius's staff has to know that Lily and I were here. Won't they recognize you two; know you're not with Aton?"

"A lot will, but not all. But you're right, Hero. It's our best chance. The odds are in our favor even if they aren't as good as I'd like. Let's go." And with that Hazel triggered the mechanism to open the door, and we slipped inside.

There was a heavy curtain secreting the door from the rest of the room. Carefully, Hazel pulled back the edge just a smidge so she could peer out into the office.

"Ok," she whispered to us as she drew the curtain back.

We tread delicately upon the floor as though afraid of triggering a land mine. My nerves were on edge. At any moment I expected a vampire to pop up and yell "Boo!"

"What are you doing here?" asked a nasal voice.

I screamed and jumped at least a foot in the air.

188

Obediah stepped out of the shadows. "Why aren't you in your room?"

"Because we didn't feel like sitting around and waiting to be killed!" I snapped.

"Obediah," Hazel said, talking over me and trying to draw the vampire's attention away from me and my rude manner. "We need to get outside. To the back of the mansion to be precise. If I can get to the balcony I believe I can cast a spell that might be helpful."

After what I'm sure was meant to be a menacing sneer at me, he turned to Hazel and said "You could go out the window."

The three of us looked quizzically at each other and then back at Obediah. "Window?" asked Lily.

He walked over to the far wall and pulled back another heavy drape revealing a window that was walled up with bricks.

"Great! We'll just go out through the window!" I cried in my best sarcastic tone, which was considerably sarcastic.

Obediah whipped his head around and snarled "Stupid human! Do you really think I'd tell you to go out the window if it were not possible?"

"It's enchanted," stated Hazel.

Before I could ask what that meant she continued "Look, Hero. It just appears to be bricked in." Hazel threw up the sash and put her arm right through the middle of the brick.

"Cool." What? What would you have said?

"This will bring you out on the right side of the building. Go around to the back," he said, pointing to the back of the mansion. The balcony you're looking for is on the far end."

"I just need to be able to see the balcony," explained Hazel.

"There's fighting going on all over the place. Won't someone notice three women suddenly appearing out of a brick wall?" Yeah, that was me being rational.

"Hang on," replied Hazel confidently. She reached into her bag of stones and rummaged for the appropriate rock. Then she muttered something while she passed the stone over her face and over the window. I had no idea what the hell she was doing.

After replacing the stone in the bag, she leaned forward and stuck her face into the imaginary brick wall. A few seconds later she straightened up and turned to us. "There's some fighting going on out there but nothing too close to the window. Just keep quiet and we'll be fine."

"Can't you do something to make us invisible or something?" Seemed a reasonable question.

"It would take up too much of my strength to do that for all three of us. I can't afford to use any more magic than necessary before I get up on that balcony."

"Oh." It never occurred to me that their magic wore out.

"I'll go first. It's a big drop so be careful." Hazel started to climb out the window.

"Uh, define 'big'?"

"About ten feet."

"What?!"

"Relax," said Lily. "Hang from your fingers and then push out hard with your feet and the palm of your hands so you don't scrape up against the side of the house."

I wanted to ask how she acquired such knowledge but decided it was a conversation best saved for another time. Instead I just nodded and hoped I appeared more confident than I felt.

"You go next, Hero. I'll follow."

Crap! I didn't want to do this. Not that I was particularly afraid of heights or anything, but I wasn't exactly fond of dropping ten feet. I poked my hand out into the bricks to test and see if it was really just a mirage. Not that I had any reason to believe otherwise, after all I'd just seen Hazel climb through the window.

"Oh, for the love of Pete! Get going!" croaked Obediah.

That did it. I'd be damned if I was going to let him get the better of me. I threw myself out of that window like I did such stunts for a living. As a reward for my hot-headedness I promptly banged the entire front of my body up against the exterior of the mansion. There were going to be some ugly bruises later.

Remembering what Lily had said, I took a deep breath and pushed away from the building, letting go of the window as I pushed. I didn't take the time to look down or even think about what I was doing. If I had I might not have had the nerve to do it. Ten feet was more of a drop than I had imagined, or maybe it just felt that way.

I landed without a single trace of gracefulness or even coordination; my body tumbling into a big lump on the grass. I suppose I should be grateful that I didn't manage to stake myself.

Barely had I time to straighten up when Lily came floating down and landed like a cat beside me. If it wasn't that bile rose in my throat at any reminder of cats, I would have been very impressed.

Shouting and growling and God only knows what other kinds of noises startled me and I quickly turned around. Two vampires were fighting furiously several yards away. Thankfully, because of the dark, they hadn't seen us.

Instinctively, we backed up against the mansion and crouched down. Hazel hissed a quiet "psst," at us and motioned for us to follow her again.

The three of us crept toward the back corner of the dwelling. Suddenly, a huge streak of gray went streaming past us followed by and even larger streak of brown. The movement was so fast it blew my hair around my face.

"Where those shifters?" I whispered.

"Yes," said Hazel.

"If they were vamps you wouldn't have seen anything at all," added Lily.

Comforting thought. I reached behind and pulled one of the make-shift stakes out of my pocket. For all the good it would do me.

When we reached the corner of the building the noise of fighting had grown even louder and more disgusting. It wasn't like when humans fight. These guys bit each other and ripped off limbs and other revolting things that made horrendously nauseating sounds.

The cold of the foundation felt good against my back. It was a nice contrast to my sweating face. I was so scared. Terrified really. What the hell were we doing? Once we got Hazel up on the balcony then what? Lily and I were practically defenseless. I know it sounds cowardly of me but really, in retrospect I wondered why we hadn't sent Hazel on alone from Darius' office. Oh, please, don't tell me you wouldn't have thought it! You probably already did. Besides, I'm here with her, so lay off.

I could see the shadows and outlines of dozens of mini battles going on across the great expanse of back lawn. The lights from the house only cast their glow so far and then the rest of the yard was reduced to obscurity. Who were they? Were any of them Kin? Was Darius out here or was he in safe keeping? No, Darius wouldn't hide. He may not be here but he was fighting somewhere. Jaeger and Mike and Angel; were they out here? Even if I were in a position to help I couldn't tell who or what I was looking at because the movements were all so incredibly fast.

"Can you see it?" asked Lily after we had taken time for our eyes to adjust to the new lighting.

"I think so. I'm not sure. The lighting, the angle. I have to get to a better position to be certain." Hazel craned her neck to try and get a better perspective of her target.

I scanned the immediate area looking for a better place for her to view the balcony. "Hazel, once you see it, how much time will you need to make your move?"

"Two or three seconds," she answered.

A vampire or a shifter could get to her in those same two or three seconds. She might have to risk it. "Do you see that chair over there, the one that's turned upside down?" I asked as I pointed to a lawn chair amid a pile of broken patio furniture. It had somehow managed to remain mostly intact. "If you can get over there you should be able to see the balcony just fine."

And therein lay the rub. She had to get over there. In the shadows up against the foundation of the mansion we were not too obvious. Of course, vamps and shifters had excellent night vision and would see us immediately if they started to look around for a new target, but as long as they were

194

otherwise engaged we were safe. However, if we went out into the light, that was another kettle of fish. Would Hazel be enough of a temptation for any of the creatures to leave their current prey and go after her instead?

Hazel reached into her pouch and took out her travel stone. "I'll have to try," she said bravely.

"Wait!" I cried, well, not cried really. More of whispered harshly. "Can you use your stone to just pop over to that spot rather than run?" Maybe it was a stupid question but even though we were just talking about a matter of a few feet at least no one would see her moving.

She and Lily looked at each other and then at me. I wasn't sure if I'd just been brilliant or incredibly stupid. Then Hazel nodded at us, warned us to be careful and disappeared. Apparently, I was brilliant.

Lily and I hastily directed our attention to the upturned lawn chair. An instant later Hazel appeared crouched down next to it. I released a breath I hadn't realized I was holding. The red haired faerie paused just long enough to glance at us over her shoulder before she disappeared again.

"Do you think she made it?" I asked.

"Of course," Lily affirmed with a determined nod.

"Now what?" I hated to ask but I knew we couldn't stay here all night either. I saw Lily look down at the collection of travel stones. I knew there was no way she could manage getting both of us out of there. In fact, she'd be damn lucky to get herself out of there.

"Go on," I told her. "I'll hide somewhere. Get yourself someplace safe."

She started to protest but I quieted her by gently pressing my fingertip to her lips. "We can't both travel on your stones and if we stay together the risk of being seen is greater. Go. Be safe. If you can manage it, go someplace where you can send help, but at least get out of harm's way." I stopped and looked around, my eyes now used to the dark. "I'll go hide over there," I declared pointing to a group of trees near the high brick wall surrounding the mansion.

Again Lily tried to protest, but I knew that she was far too weak to be able to fight if we were discovered and I would be lucky to defend myself if I had to, let alone try and defend us both. "Go!" I urged her one more time before I turned and dashed toward the trees.

Chapter 15

"Holy crap, holy crap, holy crap," I muttered under my breath as I ran. Yeah, I know, it seems a stupid thing to do but I needed something to focus on besides the distance to the trees. Never underestimate the power of distracting your own mind from unpleasant thoughts. That's much deeper than it seems. Trust me.

I threw myself behind a large oak tree, clinging to its rough bark for dear life and praying I hadn't been seen. Burying my nose and mouth into my hands, I tried to slow my breathing so my panting wouldn't alert some super-hearing being that I was in close proximity.

Would they hear the hammering of my heart anyway? Smell my nervous perspiration? Sense my presence no matter what I did? This train of thought was not doing anything for my heart rate.

I looked up searching for a limb or branch to grab onto. They were all far too high for me to reach. Twisting, I anxiously looked at the other trees nearby and noticed all of their limbs and branches were also too high for me to reach. Really? For crying out loud! How were kids supposed to climb trees if there wasn't anything they could reach? What was the world coming to?

Gauging the distance between the wall and the tree I deliberated trying to stretch between the two in order to gain some height. Unfortunately, my legs were too short to make that work. And once again, the entire Universe was conspiring against me. And again, I was not flattered by the attention.

The snarls and cries of creatures battling in the dark seemed to be inching ever closer. I felt tears well in my eyes and my throat tightened. Damn it! I longed to cry out for help and have someone rescue me, but it disgusted me to admit it, even to myself.

I peered through the darkness to see if Lily had managed to get herself out of there. There was no sign of her. I hoped that meant she was safe. And what about my other faerie friend? Was Hazel's spell-casting successful? What spell was she casting anyway? What was it supposed to do? Why didn't I ask? I had no way of knowing whether she had cast it or not, or if it was working.

Suddenly, the hair on the back of my neck stood up. I shivered and felt nauseous. Someone, or something, was behind me.

Slowly, I turned to see a dark haired vampire smiling at me. Blood was smeared across his face and dripped from his fangs. I had never seen him before but he seemed to know who I was, or at least that I was on the other side.

My back was against the tree; I had nowhere to go. I couldn't outrun him and I sure as hell couldn't fight him off.

Remember the part where I just said I couldn't outrun him? That didn't stop me from trying. Sadly, I only got one or two steps in any direction before he blocked my way. Not that he seemed to mind. On the contrary, he enjoyed it. I felt like a mouse being toyed with by a cat.   A big dark, bloody cat. Oh man, I really hated cats!

We danced back and forth.   Graceful as ever, I managed to trip a few times and even ran right into the tree. Finally having enough, the creature's smile broadened and he leapt at me. Just in the nick of time I grabbed a stake from my back pocket and raised it.   The vampire impaled himself on it, erupting blood all over me in great spurts. Unable to control myself, I screamed, stupidly, for not only did I make my position known to everyone and everything in the vicinity, but I got a mouth full of vampire blood.

I pushed him back off of me and he staggered a bit before falling on the grass. I wasn't completely sure that he was fully dead; again. Spitting blood out of my mouth, I took a step towards the body and stamped on the stake with all my might, making sure it was imbedded as far as it would go.

Wiping my tongue on my shirtsleeve, I looked around frantically, waiting to see who or what would attack me next. But I never saw him coming.

Before I knew what was happening, I had been swept up and launched into the branches I had been so longing to scale just moments before. A hand was clasped over my mouth to keep me from screaming again. When we stopped moving I was able to see my abductor and was glad beyond all reason to discover that it was Angel.

Without thinking I threw my arms around him and said "Why is it whenever a vampire starts bleeding all over me, you show up to save me?"

He smiled and put a finger to his lips to caution me to be quiet. He took off his jacket and wrapped it around my shoulders. "Stay still, stay quiet," he whispered. "I will send someone back to get you out of here." And then he was gone.

I felt like Jane left alone in a treetop by Tarzan. I wanted to ask why he couldn't get me out of there, but not only had there not been time, but it would have seemed ungrateful.

And I was grateful, very grateful. Glad to be hidden in the branches, glad to have his jacket to help keep me warm, especially since my shirt was soaked with blood. Ugh, yuck! Ok, Hero, try not to think about that one.

You might think it would be hard not to think about the fact that your shirt is completely saturated with the blood of a vampire that tried to kill you, but when there are plenty of his pals still lurking about it's amazing how easy you can get your mind off of it.

Gingerly, I turned myself so that my back was against the tree trunk. I pulled up my knees and wrapped my arms around myself. Then I closed my eyes and strained to focus all my energy on thinking of nothing more than the tree: The feel of the bark; the scent of the budding leaves and Angel's soap from his jacket; the gentle rustle when the breeze blew through the branches.

'Just you and the tree, Hero. There's nothing else here. Just you and the tree,' I repeated in my head over and over again.

Picture it: A vampire that you staked is oozing whatever is left of his after-life all over the lawn below you while you are stuck, perched in a large oak tree with no means of getting down (other than falling, not really an option). You are drenched in blood and can hear the sounds of people and creatures battling and doing horrendous things to one another all around you with no end in sight. Virtually helpless, you are left to hide in a tree waiting for the arrival of you-know-not-who, who will hopefully deliver you to safety, but since you don't know all the players in this little war you can't be sure what team the next being you see will be playing for. Hardly the making of one of Mastercard's 'Priceless' commercials.

With little else to do at this moment, I decided to examine the chain of events that led me here. And it all came down to one thing. I got picked up by a vampire at my 30th birthday celebration.

Kin. It was all simply because I had smiled at Kin and alcohol had given me the nerve to go up and talk to him at that nightclub. Well that's it! I'm never drinking again! If I get out of here, that is. Well, either way I guess.

What the hell was Kin thinking getting involved with a human when he knows that all these supernatural freaks will use anyone he gets close to as leverage in their stupid games? Selfish bastard! Why didn't he stick to his own kind?

Oh God! Had I actually just thought that? Ewww. Didn't like that. Not at all. Sighing, I pulled my arms tighter around my knees. Never really thought about the fact that you could be a bigot where supernatural beings were concerned. Then again, until a few weeks ago, I didn't know supernatural beings were real.

It wasn't Kin's fault really. After all, he just wants to find love like any of us do. And it's not like he asked to become a vampire. He had his whole life torn from him, including his mother. I shivered as I recalled how it felt to have vampires bite into you against your will. No, I couldn't blame Kin. Especially now that I had some small idea of what he had suffered.

So, who was to blame for all this crap? For my life being in jeopardy again, and again over the course of just a few short weeks? Was there any one person to blame?

Regardless of who was to blame, the fact of the matter was, if I got out of this alive, future threats to my life would have to be on my head if I chose to stay with Kin. I knew now that the encounter with Leontine was not so out of the ordinary.

I sighed again, feeling melancholy.

"Tch, so sad. What a shame. And I thought you would be so happy to see me again."

My blood ran cold and my breath caught in my chest. I didn't want to open my eyes and look up, but I couldn't help myself.

Aton was perched at the other end of the limb with a sublimely happy smile upon his face. I looked down at the ground below. Surely it would be preferable to fall and break my neck than let him kill me, but would he catch me before I could fall to my death?

"Nowhere to go, Miss Fletcher," he said as though reading my mind.

"Nothing better to do? Or are you going after little fish like me to keep yourself safe from the big fish out there?" Yeah, I know, but once again, the only weapon I have is sarcasm and the ability to annoy and irritate. What would you prefer I do? Just sit there quietly and wait to die? Oh, hell no!

He chuckled. It was a horrible sound. "No, no. Finding you was merely a happy accident."

"I wish you'd meet another happy accident," I cracked before I knew what I was saying.

Aton scowled at me now, his brows furrowing deeply. "Insolent insect! Are you too ignorant even to know when you should be afraid? Terribly, terribly afraid?" His voice rose and he began to creep closer.

Completely unbidden, the thought that filled my mind was 'Where's a banana peel when you really need one?' I couldn't help myself. In my distressed and panicked state, I began to laugh. Heaven help me, I couldn't stop! I laughed uncontrollably as though it were the most hysterically funny thing in the history of humor. And yes, I'm fully aware that it wasn't that funny at all, but there's no accounting for what the mind will do under such circumstances.

Needless to say, Aton was beyond furious. His nostrils flared angrily and eyes bulged. "How dare you! How dare you!" he raged. He tried to stand in order to be even more menacing, but my laughter was rocking the branch.

"I have had enough of you, human! You will taunt me no more!" And still, I could not control my laughter.

Aton reached for me, his long, dark fingers about to curl around my ankle, when a sudden flash and whoosh of air knocked him out of the tree and nearly took me with him.

Below me I could see Kin fighting with Aton. Kin had gotten a good strike in when he surprised him in the tree, but Aton was so much older and stronger. The pair battled back and forth under the tree. It was often hard to see them at all because they moved so swiftly. Sometimes I feared they had left the area.

After many, many minutes of combat, Aton threw Kin up against the trunk of an opposite tree and knocked the wind out of him. For an instant the fighting stopped.

Aton laughed evilly; enjoying the win he believed would soon be his. While Aton was distracted, Kin looked up at me to assure me that he was ok and I signaled for him to stay put. He looked quizzically at me, but stayed.

Carefully, I shifted into a crouching position and drew the second stake from my back pocket, now very glad that I had ignored the discomfort of it when I had first sat down.

I waited while Aton slowly advanced on Kin, gloating over his imagined victory. Once he was directly below me, I leapt from the tree, hoping to Christ I didn't miss or impale myself on the stake.

I landed square on Aton as I'd hoped, but unfortunately, the stake went into his upper shoulder instead of his heart.

Desperately, I tried to pull the stake out so I could plunge it through his back and into his heart, but the ancient vampire threw me off.

He stood and cried out in a combination of anguish and rage. He turned and pounced on me, knocking all of the air out of me. His knees thrust into my torso and felt more like pillars of cement than body parts of another being. Roughly, he grabbed my head with his left hand and my shoulder with his right and pushed them apart to make room to sink his teeth into my neck.

Thank God, Kin rushed forward, withdrew the stake from his shoulder and thrust it straight through his heart, coming out the other side.

Aton gaped in horror and amazement at the point of the stake. With whatever was left in him he croaked, "You," with all the disgust he could manage and then threw himself at my throat, covering me in a fresh coat of vampire blood.

Kin pulled him off of me and then gathered me up in his arms. "Hold on," he said unnecessarily.

I buried my head against his shoulder and closed my eyes as he ran with me to safety. When he finally put me down, we were in Darius' office. I couldn't have been more surprised.

My surprise obviously showed. "It's ok, just hang on," Kin assured me as he sat beside me, holding my hand.

Suddenly, there was a loud voice that raised above all the sounds of violence within and without the mansion.

"Cease fighting immediately. Aton has met the Final Death. I repeat, Aton has met the Final Death. All fighting will cease immediately. Take your wounded and leave."

"What?" I asked Kin in shock. "Are you kidding me? That's it? All those vampires and shifters and faes and God-knows what else that opposed Darius get to just walk away?"

"Shh. Don't worry," Kin assured me in a soft whisper. "You can bet Darius knows exactly who opposed him and who stood by him. But he also knows who was forced or coerced to side with Aton. Now is not the time to sort all of that out. For now, he wants to see to the wounded."

Well, you could have knocked me over with a feather. Whoever would have believed Darius would put the needs of the wounded ahead of everything else?

I sat back and was soon reminded of my horrifically bloody state. Except for a few tiny spots here and there, the only part of my shirt that wasn't crimson was on the back. Dark streaks that looked more black now than red had seeped into my jeans and splatters of various shapes and sizes adorned the recently-white sneakers.

God! I wanted out of that shirt! My bra was probably blood-soaked as well. That was a lovely thought! Was there any delicate way to ask for a clean shirt, or at least a reasonably cleaner shirt, under the circumstances?

Kin's shirt was torn and blood spattered but vastly cleaner than mine. If only he had an undershirt on beneath it! At least then I could ask him for it, but I couldn't very well leave him standing there topless. Well, I guess I could, but that would be sort of awkward. Or would it? Was shirtlessness among male vampires an issue? More importantly, was this the time to find out?

That left Obediah and a pair of vampires I didn't know, neither of which were dressed in layers anyway. Great, out of options. I certainly didn't want to wait for any more vampires to join the party and see if there were any candidates for clothes swapping. Something had to give now. I felt like a blood-covered human-cicle, and I was the very last one the Vampire Good Humor Man had. I didn't want to wait around to see who was going to get to enjoy a tasty treat!

"Psst," I hissed at Kin. "Hide me behind a curtain or something for a minute."

"What?"

"Just do it!" I urged as I grabbed his arm and pulled him towards the hidden window that Hazel, Lily and I had disappeared through earlier.

I popped behind the curtain and whispered, "Stay there and keep guard!"

"Guard? Hero, what are you doing?" he asked nervously.

"Getting out of the bloody shirt!"

With no other option readily available, I shed the disgusting garment, make that garments. The bra was as nasty as I had feared. Don't ask me why but somehow that was more sickening than the shirt. Then I put Angel's coat back on over my naked torso and zipped it all the way up. Hope he didn't have his heart set on getting it back tonight.

Stepping out from behind the curtain, I shoved the bundle of blood-soaked rags into Kin's hands. "Find a place to get rid of those please?"

Kin raised first one eyebrow and then the other as he looked back and forth from the lump of gory cloth to the jacket. "Wh-what..."

"It's Angel's jacket. He gave it to me when he took me up into the tree."

"Um, yeah, but,"

"But, nothing. And I mean 'nothing'. I couldn't bear to have *them* on me a minute longer," I said, pointing to the bundle in his hand, "and I had nothing else to put on."

I couldn't tell if it was just the thought of me standing there with nothing on under the jacket or that I was naked underneath Angel's jacket that was the problem, and frankly, I didn't give a rat's ass one way or the other.

Kin opened his mouth to say something else but I rushed in. "Unless you have something else that I can put on, please just let it go. After everything that's happened tonight, actually, after the past several days, this really isn't worth arguing about."

Good man, he agreed and kissed me on the forehead. "I'll get rid of these. Go sit on the couch and I'll see if I can find out about Hazel and Lily for you, ok?"

Very good man. Aside from offering to get me chocolate, that was the best possible thing he could have said to me.

As I sat on the couch I marveled that I could sit there so calmly after all that had taken place. I should be a complete wreck, a total basket case! Had I had a nervous breakdown and just didn't know it? Did that happen?

But it was all so surreal. I'd been kidnapped by vampires and tortured. Then they kidnapped a friend of mine who happens to be a faerie and took us to the headquarters of a rival group of super-naturals. My God! Am I actually writing this? Just putting down on paper seems insane let alone claiming that it actually happened. And I'm not done yet!

Then the fae and I were imprisoned and discovered that we were betrayed by another fae. Wait a minute? Why am I summing up? You've been here all the time. This is unnecessary and redundant.

The hell with that! So, after everything I had been through – and you know what I mean – why the hell wasn't I having a major freak out? Or at least a minor freak out?

I was sitting on a couch in Darius' luxurious office with Obediah and two strange vampires, waiting to hear what had happened to my faerie friends during the battle. I might as well have been waiting for afternoon tea at the Four Seasons in Boston.

Oddly, inexplicably calm. Perhaps it was the knowledge that Aton was dead and that he couldn't hurt me, or anyone else, again. Yes, there was a certain amount of satisfaction in that.

The secret door opened at the back of the office and three more vampires entered. One of them looked familiar. I had probably seen him in the anteroom at some point, but the other two were strangers.

They stopped in their tracks and looked strangely at me. "McIntyre," stated Obediah simply. The trio nodded and moved over to talk to the pair who had already been conversing in the corner.

I was feeling terribly outnumbered and in need of a friendly face. Then the front door of the office swung open and Darius came striding in with Jaeger and a party of particularly serious looking vampires on his heels. I had to say, while it was obvious Darius had been in an altercation of some kind, he didn't look much the worse for the wear. Perhaps it was a vampire thing. His normally impeccable clothes were a bit rumpled and there were a few strands of hair rakishly out of place, but if it weren't for the bits of blood spattered here and there and the small tear in his shirt, you might not have known anything had taken place.

Turning to address his crew, he caught site of me and paused. "Oh, Miss Fletcher! I hadn't been made aware that you were here. If you would please," It was obvious from his expression and the way he indicated with the sweep of his arm that he was about to send me off to the anteroom. Wasn't happening.

"Please forgive me, Magistrate, but after all that I've been through, and seeing that I was one of those directly responsible for killing Aton, I hope you will please allow me to wait here for Kin to return and not send me out there among strangers in my weakened condition."

Nervy, yes, but I doubt even Darius was surprised by this time.

"You were responsible for Aton meeting his true death?" he asked, making no effort to hide his shock.

"Yes. I jumped on him from behind and attempted to stake him, but I hit too high. When he turned to attack me, Kin quickly removed the stake and, well, I'm sure you know how it turned out." I lived it. I didn't need to relive it blow by blow.

"I see."

Did he? Did I care? Not really. I just didn't want to go out into the huge waiting area with a fair amount of blood still on me and nothing on underneath Angel's jacket.

I tried to make eye contact with Jaeger. I still hadn't had a chance to talk to him since this whole nightmare began. Call me crazy, but I really wanted to talk to him about the day I had been abducted and tell him I know it wasn't his fault.

"I am grateful, Miss Fletcher, to you and to Kinley for your bravery and efficiency. However, there are things we must discuss that I am afraid you cannot be present for. I must ask you to leave."

Oh crap! "I understand. May I please request that I be shown to a room instead of waiting out there then?"

"Of course," he replied smoothly. "I will have Sadir show you to your room and Kinley will be made aware of your arrangements."

"Oh, um. Not the Vienna room again." Damn! That came out all wrong. Quick, Hero, cover up! "I, uh, have bad associations with that room. You know, being so worried and all. It wouldn't be restful." I blurted out like a babbling idiot. I could hardly tell him I didn't want to go back there because we'd trashed it.

A few eyebrows were raised and a few furrowed, but nobody said a word. Darius merely smiled politely and nodded. "Sadir!"

Then I remembered. "Wait! Um, sorry. Forgive me, Dar-Magistrate. Hazel and Lily. Are they alright?"

Had to give him credit. He tried so hard not to look exasperated with me. "Yes, Miss Fletcher. They are both fine. They are resting. I'm not certain if the doctor has seen to them yet, but there are a lot of patients requiring his attention this evening."

"Yes, naturally. Thank you." I nearly asked about Angel and Mike but had the sense to bite my tongue and follow the large, silent Sadir out of the office.

Chapter 16

Sadir marched me through the crowd of bloody and beleaguered vampires. Many turned their heads to watch us pass, but most ignored us, intent on sharing glorious tales of victory with their peers.

The main hallway was dotted with pairs and small groupings of people. Well, vampires, whatever. The overflow from the anteroom who hung in the wings to wait for any news.

What kind of news were they waiting for? Casualties? The state of relations with Ilderim and his menagerie? I was too worn out to waste energy on any more supernatural political intrigue.

Sadir took me up the staircase where I had stayed on a previous occasion; the time I came here with Lily after I had defeated Leontine. I wondered if this was where those in need of attention from Dr. Galeno generally stayed.

"Excuse me, Sadir. By any chance, will I be staying near Hazel or Lily?"

"I could make that so if you wished," he replied kindly. His voice was deep and rich.

"Thank you, Sadir. That's very considerate of you."

213

We had only just reached to top of the staircase and paused on the first landing. "Would you like me to show you to your room first or would you prefer to go directly to your friends?"

I had to admit I was floored by his polite and respectful manner. This was the stoic guard that was always so intimidating. It seemed like there had to be two of them and now I was talking to the nice twin and it was the evil twin who normally guarded Darius.

"I would like to see my friends, please. Thank you."

He nodded and then led me to the right end of the hallway. "You will find your friends in here," he said as he paused at the third doorway on the left. "Your room will be the one diagonally opposite. I will leave the door ajar and a light on for you."

"Thank you again, Sadir. I appreciate your help." He nodded one last time and then walked past me to take care of my room.

I knocked softly on the bedroom door. "Come in," called Hazel.

I opened the door gently and poked my head through. "May I come in?"

"Hero! Come in, come in!" Hazel cried happily, as relieved to see me as I was to see her.

She was sitting propped up in a large bed and had been reading a book. Next to her, Lily was curled up in a ball fast asleep.

"Oh," I whispered when I noticed Lily. I was afraid we'd wake her up.

"Don't worry. She'll be out for hours. Poor thing."

"Poor thing? What happened? Is she ok?" Oh crap! I left her alone! Did something happen to her?

"She's fine, Hero. It's ok. She's just completely drained. Using those travel stones took everything she had left in her. Obediah said when she showed up he thought she was dead at first. She appeared in an unconscious heap. But it was just that it sapped her completely."

"But she'll be ok?" I still wasn't sure things called for the cavalier attitude Hazel seemed to have.

"Oh, yeah. She's going to need a lot of rest and it's going to be a long time before she's got her strength back." Hazel looked at her friend and watched her sleeping with a sad, pitying look upon her face.

"She won't ever be herself again though, will she?" I felt the bile rise in my throat just saying it.

"No," she replied in a small voice.

"The stones?"

Hazel just nodded.

I don't know why, but I had hoped somehow when Aton died the stones would be returned to Lily, but who knew where they were or what he had done to them? I didn't dare voice that to Hazel though. I knew it was too sensitive a subject.

"How about you? Were you hurt?"

She shook her mop of shocking red hair. "Un uh. Fought off a pair of shifters who tried to get me off the balcony, but..." She let her sentence trail off.

We lapsed into an awkward silence. I hate awkward silences. Well, it's not like anyone actually likes them, but you know what I mean. Thankfully, a knock came on the door.

"Come in," called Hazel as she had for me.

Kin stepped in and smiled at us. "I hope I'm not intruding."

"No, of course not. I'm glad to see you, Kin," answered Hazel genuinely.

He went to her bedside and squeezed her hand. "Your spell-work was wonderful, Hazel. Thank you. You really made a difference."

She blushed adorably and thanked him. "All that matters is that Aton was beaten."

"Thanks to Hero," Kin replied.

"Thanks to you, actually," I corrected.

"What?" Hazel asked, sitting upright. "Hero? What happened?"

"Nothing," I replied before Kin could answer. "I jumped on him from behind and tried to stake him but I missed. Then when Aton turned on me, Kin pulled out the stake and killed him."

Her eyes were like saucers. "That's it. You just... staked him?"

"What should we have done? Drawn and quartered him?" Not that that was a bad idea.

"No, it's just... he was so... I...," Hazel was at a loss for words.

"I know what you mean, Hazel." Kin shoved his hands in his pockets and walked to the end of the bed. "It seems like it was just too easy, doesn't it? I keep going over it in my head, but that *is* what happened and he *is* gone."

"Sooo..... what?" I didn't like this. "Are you saying he's not really dead or something?" I felt myself beginning to panic. It was like a Halloween or Friday the 13th movie where even though you know you killed the psycho, it keeps coming back!

"No, no. He's met his true death. I just don't understand how?"

217

"What do you mean? You staked him?"

"Hero, this was a very old vampire who thrived on fighting. And yet, it was as though his guard was completely down."

"Well, Hazel, what kind of spells were you doing? Could that have done something to him?"

She shrugged. "I did cast a spell to weaken and confuse my enemies, but that only works on those who are my direct enemies."

"Well, wasn't he? He tried to kill both me and Lily? He kidnapped me from your house? Wouldn't that make him your enemy?"

"It's normally someone who has done something directly to me. But, I suppose. He was on my land when he took you. And Lily is my closest friend."

"And he stole Lily's stones. If stealing the stones from your best friend doesn't make someone your enemy I don't know what would."

"Yes, that's true," she replied through clenched teeth as she looked down again at the sleeping form of Lily.

"I suppose," added Kin, "that Aton was a threat to your whole tribe really. And certainly that would make him your enemy. I don't know if any of your other tribesmen were also casting spells tonight, but if they were casting ones like you were against your enemies, I suppose that could account for his lack of skill and attentiveness."

218

"I really don't know. I'm certain that there were other members of my tribe here this evening, but I don't know what spells may have been cast or by whom, but I suppose it's possible."

"Oh, great!" I cried in exasperation.

Kin and Hazel looked at me quizzically. "Well, now we've got another vampire who's been defeated and to the outside world, correction, the outside supernatural world, it will seem he was defeated too easily. Please tell me that Aton's maker is not still alive and will be coming to avenge his true death?"

Hazel's eyes widened to almost impossible dimensions while I spouted off. I knew she was afraid I might spill the beans about how Mike defeated Nigel, but she needn't worry. I would take that to the grave. And I nearly had.

"Aton's maker has been dead for centuries."

I wasn't sure how Kin knew that. I suppose it was the norm to be familiar with famous vampire pedigrees.

"So, no one is going to come looking to investigate the all-too-easy demise of Aton?"

"I don't imagine they will, but I will make sure Darius knows of the importance of the fae spells and that that information is freely shared."

Another knock at the door kept me from thanking him. This time it was Dr. Galeno. "Good evening everyone," he said as he entered the room.

"Miss Greenleaf, how are you feeling?"

"I'm doing well, thank you, Doctor. Just a few minor cuts and scrapes."

"Good," he said as he placed his medical bag on the nightstand. "And your friend is still sleeping soundly?"

"Oh, yes. She's out like a light," Hazel informed him as she smiled at Lily.

"Excellent. Best thing for her."

"Miss Fletcher," he said as he looked over his shoulder at me. "If you will please retire to your room, I shall attend your injuries momentarily."

"My injuries?" I looked incredulously from him, to Kin to Hazel and back again.

"Yes, Miss Fletcher. Unless I am very much mistaken, in addition to many cuts and scrapes of your own, you have some cracked ribs and a swollen ankle."

"Get out of here! I think I'd know if I had cracked my ribs and my ankle is fine," I declared, raising my foot in the air so everyone could see my perfectly fine, yet somewhat inflated ankle.

"Oh." I looked at Kin sheepishly. Suddenly I was afraid to move in case I really had hurt my ribs and had been too pumped up on adrenaline to feel it. Now that it had been brought to my attention, I'd feel it, and I didn't want to.

"Why don't you go get some rest, Hero. I'll see you in the morning," said Hazel, trying to help.

Dr. Galeno smiled at me kindly. "I won't be long, dear."

"Come on," said Kin as he turned me and led me out the door.

As we made our way to the room diagonally opposite, I was loathe to admit that I was sore and uncomfortable on both of my sides.

"How can I have cracked ribs and not know? And how the hell can he know?"

"Let's just get you cleaned up and in bed and worry about it later."

"Later? My ribs are cracked *now*! I'm shuffling behind you like Tim Conway as the Little Old Man because I'm afraid to move more freely than that! Cleaned up and into bed? I don't even know if I can climb into bed!"

Ok, so I was starting to freak out a little bit. What? Like you wouldn't freak out a bit? Give me a break. I think all things considered, I've held on to my freak pretty damned well.

"Let me carry you," he offered, reaching to pick me up.

"No! Don't touch me! That might hurt more!" I cried coming to a complete halt and wrapping my arms around myself.

"Ok," he said, backing off. "I won't carry you. Hero, I know that cracked ribs hurt, but Dr. Galeno will be in to see you very soon and I promise he will take good care of you. Let's just get you in there, out of those bloody clothes and into bed."

I felt silly. But we all have our limits and right now I was pushing mine. Pain was not something I could handle well at the moment. All my bravado was used up.

Grimacing what I hoped looked like a positive sort of smirk, I nodded and shuffled past him at a glacial pace and eventually made it into the bedroom.

True to his word, Sadir had left the room ready for me. The lamp was on next to the bed. The bed was turned down and there was a clean nightgown folded on the bed.

Once again I wondered at the readiness of clothing at the mansion. Then, because I was tired, and now sore, I crabbily remembered my first night here and that there had not been any clean clothes or any amenities for me then. I sighed. Let it go, Hero. You've got enough on your plate.

Kin led me to the bed and I sat down gingerly. He stooped and took off my shoes and socks. Then he reached for the nightgown and shook it out.

"Do you need help taking off the jacket?"

"I don't think so," I answered as I pulled down the zipper. "Oh! Angel! Kin, are Angel and Mike ok?"

"They're going to be fine."

222

"Going to be?" I repeated with concern.

"They both had some minor injuries, nothing serious. They'll both be back to normal by morning."

I breathed a sigh of relief as I let Angel's jacket fall off my shoulders. "What about you? Does Dr. Galeno need to see you for anything?"

He smiled at me. "No, thankfully. All of my wounds were superficial enough to heal fine on their own." He held up the nightgown for me to put my arms in.

"So, what's going to happen now? With Ilderim and all the members of his menagerie and stuff?"

"And "stuff"?" he parroted with a smile.

I winced and let out a little grunt of pain as I pulled the nightgown down over my head and shoulders.

"Are you ok?" he asked, his turn to show concern.

"Yup," I said with more confidence than I felt.

Steadying myself with my hands on his shoulders, I stood and let him unfasten my jeans and pull them down over my legs. Then I sat back down on the edge of the bed as he tugged them off over my feet, careful not to hurt my swollen ankle.

"Well?' I asked, doing my best to be patient.

"Well?" he replied, clearly forgetting our previous train of conversation.

"Stuff?"

"Oh! Yeah, Ilderim. I don't really know what's going to happen there. I know Aton used a great deal of undue influence and duress to get people to fight for him."

"Like kidnapping people's family members?"

"I'm not certain, but I wouldn't be surprised. It's going to take some time to figure out who went willingly and who was forced. And, there's no telling how Darius will feel about those who were forced."

"What do you mean?"

"He might feel that they should have chosen death rather than betrayal."

"What? But death of a loved one? Of someone innocent?"

"Not everyone who was forced was forced because of threats against a loved one, Hero."

I didn't know what to say to that. I was sorry I had asked.

Thankfully, just then, there was a knock on the door. Kin let Dr. Galeno in and he came straight over to me and placed his bag on the nightstand.

"Now then, let's have a look at that ankle."

So much for small talk. Then again, I had no idea how many other people he had left to see before he called it a night.

Like a good girl I raised my left leg and let him inspect my ankle. His touch was very light and I barely knew he was examining me at all. I can't tell you how thankful I was for that.

When he was done with the ankle, he instructed me to get under the covers and raise the nightgown so he could see my torso. With vampire speed, Kin was suddenly between us, helping me lie back, covering me up to my waist and then delicately working my nightgown up until my ribs were exposed for the Dr. to examine. Like this ancient physician to the supernatural was trying to get a peek at me! If it wouldn't have hurt my ribs, I would have laughed. On second thought, it was kind of sweet that Kin was so protective. I decided I was glad it was too painful to laugh.

Just as gentle with the ribs as he was with the ankle, Dr. Galeno made a quick study of my injuries and then pulled my nightgown down over my stomach. "It will just take a moment to mix your draught," he said as he smiled at me kindly.

Thinking of the other times I'd seen him give potions to my friends, I remembered my new necklace. "Dr.? Will this make any difference, or is that just for faeries?"

He turned to see what I was talking about and raised his eyebrows when he saw the gift I'd been given. "Well, my, my, my!" He reached for it and held it carefully, inspecting the stones. "Yes, a very special gift indeed. Very special. I'm glad you showed this to me." He winked at me and turned back to his potion making.

When he was done, he held up a crystal vial that contained a pale red liquid. Not pink, red. But still pale. I tried to make myself think of Vick's 44 and not blood, but considering my surroundings, it was difficult.

Then he lifted my necklace, clicked the vial against each of the three stones while he muttered some words that sounded like gibberish to me.

I watched in amazement as the once red liquid became purple and then blue and finally a light aqua, the color people think water should be, but of course it isn't.

He handed me the crystal vessel. I removed the stopper and lifted it to my lips. Bracing myself, I took a deep breath and poured the contents into my mouth, swallowing as quickly as I could. Strangely, I found it had no taste whatsoever.

"There now. You get some rest and you'll be fine in the morning."

"Thank you, Dr." I said as I handed the vial back to him.

Once he had gone, Kin came and sat on the side of the bed. "How do you feel?"

"Tired, actually." And I did. I felt so very tired. I wondered if it had anything to do with the good doctor's medicine.

Kin smiled at me. "Get some sleep." He reached up to fluff the pillows and make me comfortable.

"You're going to stay here with me, aren't you?" Ugh! There was that stupid damsel thing again. The danger was over, what did I care if he left?

"I'll be back, but there are some things I want to check on. I won't be leaving the mansion," he added, as though that made it better.

I wanted to protest; to pout and be childish and tell him to stay here with me. And don't think I wouldn't have, but I was so overcome with sleepiness that I couldn't even muster a halfway decent pout let alone a protest. The last thing I remembered was Kin kissing my forehead and promising to be back very soon. I never even heard him leave.

Chapter 17

There's one good thing about sleeping at a mansion owned by a vampire. (Boy! That's something I never thought I'd hear myself say!) You don't get woken up by the sun shining in your eyes in the morning.

Yeah, I know. The sun isn't really the life and death issue we always thought it was for the Undead, but they see no reason to ever suffer even a moment of discomfort and have the resources to live that way. On this one point at least, you would never hear me complain.

Although, it is a bit disconcerting to wake up and think it must be morning and be unable to tell. Thankfully, I could read the clock clearly from my position on the bed and knew I ought to get up.

I peeled the covers back and swung my legs over the side of the bed, glad to note that the aches and pains I had subconsciously expected did not materialize. Thank you, Dr. Galeno! I padded over to the armoire and discovered clean clothes inside. I shook my head. I guess this meant I was somehow accepted by Darius or something, I don't know?

Doing my best to be a glass-half-full kind of gal, I decided to just be glad I had clean clothes and gathered them up and headed off to the bathroom for a nice hot shower.

Kin scared the living hell out of me sometime later when I suddenly noticed his reflection in the mirror while drying my hair, resulting in a blood-curdling scream and a broken hairdryer.

"What the hell are you doing?" I shrieked at him in indignation. "Ever hear of knocking?"

"Why yes, I've heard of it, but you couldn't hear it." Smart ass. You'd think he'd know better, wouldn't you.

I glared at him with all the fury I could muster, and I was feeling more myself than I had in several days, so there was a lot of mustering going on. "That's not funny. Do you really think sneaking up on me like that, especially after the events of the last few days, was a nice thing to do?"

"I wasn't trying to sneak up on you. I called your name, but you couldn't hear me."

"So why not just sit down and wait in the room? Why come and hover over me in the bathroom?"

He shrugged. "I just wanted you to know I was here."

Men! Even when they're over one hundred years old they still act like children.

"Well, you're going to explain that to Darius," I said angrily, pointing at the smashed hairdryer lying in pieces on the floor.

Kin smiled at it; he nearly laughed. "Not to worry."

I suddenly wished that hairdryer was whole again so I could smash it over his smug head! Oh what? Please! He's a vampire! Like it would do any damage to him. Even if it cut him, he'd heal in seconds. I'd be more likely to hurt myself doing it than hurt him, so chill out.

Sensing that I was formulating ways to vent my frustration on him, Kin chose to do his first clever thing of the day. "Would you like to go get some breakfast?"

For once my stomach didn't give me away by growling. I thrust out my chin and replied "Do you think I'm going to forgive you that easily?"

Kin smiled at me again, but this time it was a tender and loving smile. No smugness in sight. "If I say I'm sorry and promise you bacon will you forgive me?"

He said the magic word! And my stomach told him so by emitting a loud growl. We both laughed and Kin joked "I'll take that as a 'yes'. Come on."

"You're looking much better," he noted a little while later while I was sipping my coffee.

"Thanks. I feel better." I smiled at him over the rim of my cup. I did feel better, thank God. But I didn't feel like talking about it.

"Can we go see Hazel and Lily after I eat?"

"I'll see," he replied. "If they are free I'm sure they'd love to see you."

Oh! Hmm. I hadn't considered that they might not be free. Would Shannon be here to see them? Would they have to meet with Darius?

"Do you know if anything can be done about Lily's stones?" I asked hopefully.

Kin shook his head. "I'm sorry, Hero. I really have no idea." And he was sorry. I could tell. His tone was that of someone speaking about a friend who was going to die, but no one wants to say out loud that they won't make it.

"She'll be ok, though, won't she?"

He looked down at the snowy white tablecloth. "She'll... she'll find ways to cope with her loss."

I felt sick to my stomach. 'Ways to cope with her loss.' Lily will live, but she'll never be whole again. And it was my fault. Tears threatened to spill out and I blinked furiously to keep them at bay.

"Don't, Hero," Kin said tenderly as he reached for my hand. "It was Aton's doing, not yours. And if anyone else is to blame at all, it's Blackthorne for being so weak."

I nodded and tried to smile but I couldn't. All I could think of was the tiny little white-haired faerie curled up in a ball beside Hazel, not even aware that we were in the room. My nose and throat stung from the tears I struggled to hold in.

"Hero!" called a much-too-cheerful voice. "Kin, Hero. There you guys are!" Mike and Angel threaded through the tables in the dining area as they made their way to us.

"Oh wow, I am so glad to see that you're ok, Hero. I was wicked worried about ya."

"Thanks, Mike. That's sweet. I'm glad to see you guys are ok too." I smiled at them both, hoping I looked happier than I felt.

"Angel, thank you so much for what you did for me last night."

He held up his hand to stop me. "No need. Really. I'm glad that you are well."

"Well, I will have your jacket cleaned and get it back to you."

"That's already been taken care of," said Kin. "I took it from your room last night after you fell asleep."

"Oh! Well… good." I felt stupid. Oh well!

Angel nodded.

"I'm so happy that neither one of you got hurt," I said groping around for something to fill the silence.

"Oh we got hurt!" Mike said with a laugh. "Boy! You should have seen me! I was such a mess, man! Ha! Scratched and bitten and pulled apart, but I kicked ass!" Per usual, it was as if it had all been some marvelous carnival ride for Mike. "Oh and Angel! Dang! He was all kinds of messed up. Half his face was missing by the time it was over." Mike found this hilarious. I failed to see the humor.

I tried my best to give Kin a very subtle stink eye. He had some answering to do for telling me that my vampire pals had only suffered minor injuries.

"Well, that Dr. Galeno sure knows his stuff." I replied, still looking at Kin.

"Yup! Sure does," answered Mike, chipper as ever, oblivious to the mounting tension.

"We should go and let you finish your breakfast," interjected Angel. Somebody was picking up on my signals at least.

After saying all our goodbyes I turned to Kin and said "Well?"

"Well, what?" he replied with total innocence.

"Kin, if we are going to have a relationship, we can't have this kind of crap going on."

His eyebrows rose significantly. "And by 'crap' you mean?"

"You lying to me."

"What! I haven't lied to you."

"Half of Angel's face was torn off and you said they only suffered some minor injuries. Minor! Having half of your face torn off does not sound like a minor injury to me!"

Kin sighed wearily. "Hero, I understand that from your perspective things like that seem enormous. I really do. But you have to please try and remember that as a vampire, I know for a fact that between our own healing powers and Dr. Galeno's efforts, injuries like that heal very quickly and they would be fine by morning. You'd been through so much. I didn't want to upset you any more."

Logic is a very fickle friend. It's one thing when Logic is there to help me figure something out, but when it's helping someone else explain their way out of pissing me off, Logic is biting me on the ass.

"Fine," I replied grudgingly. I hated to admit it, but I understood why he kept it from me. I didn't like having it kept from me. Yeah, I know. I was being a moody bitch, but it was going to take some time to get me back on an even keel. You try going through everything I've been through and see how stable you are. Don't judge me.

"I have an idea," Kin announced. "Why don't you and I go away for a couple of days?"

"What? Really? Go where?" Getting away from everything for a couple of days sounded heavenly.

"I don't know? New Hampshire, Maine? Wherever you want."

I suddenly felt just a little lighter. Away. Away from the memories of Aton and Alex and Bradley. Away from the nightmare of being bitten over and over again. Away from the whole ordeal of being kidnapped, having my friend kidnapped, of being in battle – again! To just be somewhere where all I had to do was think of simply relaxing and being safe with Kin. Paradise.

My eyes filled with a different kind of tear this time. "Yes, I'd like that very much. Can we go right away? Will Darius let you?"

Kin scooted his chair around beside mine and put his arm around me. "I'm not certain just how quickly, but I'm sure we can go fairly soon." He kissed the top of my head and squeezed my shoulders. "Everything's going to be alright, Hero. I promise."

I was done being moody and negative. I let that unkeepable promise slide; refused to comment or even let my mind linger on it. Now was not the time to dwell on promises that can't be kept.

Our moment of contentment was interrupted by the not-so-subtle clearing of a throat. We looked up to see Obediah standing on the opposite side of the table looking at us as though we were something he'd scraped off the bottom of his shoe. I wasn't sure I'd ever seen anyone's nostrils arch quite so high.

"Miss Fletcher," he spat in a barely civil tone. "Miss Greenleaf requests your presence immediately."

"Oh!" I gasped. "I hope Lily's ok. Is she alright?" I foolishly asked Obediah.

He looked down his crooked, olive-skinned nose and told me "I'm sure you'll find out for yourself momentarily." What a guy.

"I'm sure she's fine. If something was wrong I doubt they'd send Obediah," Kin assured me.

I wasn't completely convinced, or entirely sure of the reason behind that statement, but I decided to go with it.

Glad that Kin was with me, because I wasn't entirely sure that I'd remember how to get to the room Hazel and Lily were in and because I would need his support if there were any bad news, we rushed off to see my faerie friends.

"Come in," Hazel called as soon as we knocked on the door.

She was sitting in a pale blue armchair that made her blazing red hair seem even brighter than normal. "Hero! How are you feeling?"

"I'm just fine. How are you? How's Lily?"

"I'm fine, just fine. Don't worry," she answered when she saw the concerned look on my face. "And Lily, she's doing as well as can be expected," she added with a smile that didn't go all the way up to her eyes. "She's having a shower," she added jerking her head toward the bathroom door.

We sat down on the sofa opposite Hazel. "Obediah said you wanted to see me."

"Yeah, I wanted to see that you were ok."

I looked at her skeptically. She wouldn't ask the disagreeable Obediah to go searching for me if it wasn't important. "Uh huh."

She knew she was caught. She grimaced at us both. "Ok." She blew out hard, eyes closed, as she steeled herself to tell us why she had sent for me.

"A messenger came a little while ago from Ilderim." She had my complete attention. "When they went through Aton's things they found Lily's stones."

"That's wonderful! That means…" My revelry was cut short by the look on Hazel's face. "What? Won't they give them back?"

Hazel reached behind her back and withdrew a drawstring bag. I recognized it immediately. "I don't understand. If Lily has her stones back she'll be fine now, won't she?"

"It's not that simple, Hero. I wish it was."

I was thoroughly confused. "Well, I don't understand. We wanted her stones back, didn't we? It's better than not getting them back, right?"

She placed the bag on the coffee table and pushed them away. "Not necessarily in this case. If they were simply taken and returned in the same condition, then yes, the faerie can almost always restore the bond. However…" she let her voice drift off.

"They aren't in the same condition, are they?" I asked, already knowing the answer.

"No," she replied quietly. "They're… These stones are strangers to her now," she choked.

I didn't understand what had happened but I realized it would pain Hazel too much to ask her to explain.

"Can I, is there any way I can help?" I stumbled awkwardly, desperate to make some offer no matter how useless.

Hazel nodded. "You can be here. You can be the friend you have been to her through all of this. She has been able to draw great strength from you."

"From me?" I interrupted in shock.

"Yes, Hero. From you. Before she went to sleep last night, Lily joked that she may have lost her stones, but you had been her rock." At that, Hazel did genuinely smile.

I didn't know how to feel about all of this. Of course I was glad that Lily felt I was helpful and knew I was there for her. But I was still dealing with feelings of being responsible for all it happening in the first place.

The bathroom door opened and Lily emerged. "Hero, Kin, how nice to see you."

"Hey, Lily. How are you feeling?"

She still looked pale though not quite as drawn as she had the past couple of days.

"Oh, I'm ok." The tiny faerie came padding over in bare feet to sit in the empty chair. Immediately she noticed the bag of stones and stopped dead in her tracks, nearly falling into her seat. Kin reached out to steady both her and the chair.

"Careful. Are you ok?" he asked?

Panting, Lily pointed at the bag. "Th-that's my... those are, are m-my stones. I know they are." Silent tears began to run down the sides of her freshly scrubbed face.

Hazel reached out and took her hand in hers. "Yes, Lily, those were your stones."

Lily's eyes widened in instant acknowledgement of what Hazel was saying. "What did he do?" she whispered.

Hazel opened her mouth to speak but her voice caught in her throat. She licked her lips and tried again. "He uh, they...," she paused and plucked at the top of the bag. "Well, we think he tried to uh, to have..."

Lily closed her eyes and groaned in pain. "He tried to ensorcel them," she moaned pitifully.

"Yes," Hazel confirmed in a tiny voice.

I wanted to ask what that meant but I knew it would be inappropriate. Don't be shocked. It happens. You guys really have to learn to have a little more faith in me.

We sat there in an uncomfortable silence for a few minutes. I'd like to note; we have a severely disproportionate number of uncomfortable silences to comfortable silences in life. Don't you think? Maybe we just don't notice the comfortable ones as much. I don't count the silences you have when you're alone because, really, what's the alternative? Talk to yourself? Then you're in line for a whole new array of uncomfortable coming at you from a bunch of well-meaning dolts who won't ever let you have a moment of silence again. Well, except when you're locked in your padded room at night.

Padded room? How did I..? Man! My mind wanders just awful sometimes.

Feeling helpless and hating it, I rose from the sofa and went to sit beside Lily on the floor. She looked at me and smiled through her tears for a moment before resuming her mournful position.

I reached out and took the bag of stones and pulled open the string. "So, nothing can be done at all?"

My red-haired friend shrugged at me. "She can try…" she began but was unable to finish.

I looked at Lily. "Can Hazel and I help in any way, Lily? Isn't there anything we can do? Anything?" I put my hand on her knee and squeezed gently.

Perhaps I was asking too much but I hated to think of her giving up after what we'd been through the past couple of days. Maybe I was too naïve or just plain ignorant, but I couldn't accept that there was no way to help.

She sniffed and wiped her eyes on the backs of her hands. "When your stones have been stolen from you there is a trauma to be worked through in order to reconnect with them. Some connections will never be the same. But when they have been touched by the magic of another creature, there is no connection. The bond is erased."

"But Aton wasn't magic?"

"Hero," Kin interjected, "to ensorcel a fae's stones means to have a witch try and enchant them to work for another."

"Oh! So, Aton sort-of tried to brainwash the stones into thinking they were his?"

Lily hiccupped what should have been a laugh. "That's one way of putting it."

I tried to process that tidbit and what exactly it meant. Had Aton merely wanted to harness the power of the stones or did he think they held some answer for him?

"Forgive me, I'm sorry. I'm just trying to understand all of this. So that means Lily's stones sort of have amnesia?"

"Sort of," replied Hazel.

"Well, sometimes people with amnesia get their memories back. Is there any way we can get her stones to get their memories back?"

Hazel shook her head.

"Even if the witch reversed her spell?" Yeah, ok. I was grasping. I'd watched too many movies.

Lily smiled at me again. "Even then."

I rooted around in the bag and pulled out a beautiful deep blue stone with dark spots on it. "Isn't this the stone you used to get all the blood off of me the night you brought me here after the battle at Leontine's?"

"Mm hm."

It was a lovely stone. Such a bright, deep blue and it felt cool in my hand. I turned it over and over and rubbed it against my palm and fingers.

"Would it hurt you to hold it?" I asked sheepishly. I didn't want to cause her pain but I was who I was. A stubborn pain in the ass who hates to give in.

I could feel the collective tension in the room after I asked her to hold the stone. You'd have thought I'd asked her to hold an ounce of raw plutonium. Maybe it was as big a deal as that, but I sure as hell didn't know.

Undeterred, I held out my hand for her to take the stone. "What kind of stone is it? Does it have a name?" I asked, hoping to deflect some of the tension.

"It's lapis. Lapis lazuli. It comes from Chile." Lily smiled at the stone while she spoke the way I might have smiled at one of my old dolls or stuffed animals. This stone was an old friend that had seen her through good times and bad and was once a source of comfort for her.

242

She picked the stone out of my hand and shuddered. Her nose wrinkled and her mouth twisted. It was as though the stone made her feel ill. But she held on.

"I remember that night," Lily said softly as she closed her hand gently around the blue stone. "I found you walking around Hazel's front yard, all alone."

"Yes," I agreed.

"The place was packed with vampires and you were covered in blood," she said with something that might have been a chuckle. "They started to smell you and realize you weren't a vampire covered in shifter blood but a human with a shifter blood coating. I had to get you cleaned up right away." She was genuinely smiling now.

"And I was totally clueless. I was oblivious to the whole situation."

"Darius was waiting," she continued, "so I couldn't leave with you. We had to stay there near the anteroom. I wasn't sure it would clean up such a big mess but it did the trick." The tiny white-haired faerie looked down lovingly at the stone in her hand. She pressed it tightly between both hands and closed her eyes.

Hazel came to sit in front of her on the floor. She took my hands and placed them on either side of Lily's. It was a bit awkward from where I was sitting, but I didn't mind.

"Think about that night. Think about being here, in the waiting room. Remember. Both of you," she said looking at me sternly. Immediately I closed my eyes. Not sure if she

243

meant that I should do that, but I felt it was the right thing to do.

"Remember," Hazel continued, "being together. The stone. Lily using the stone to cleanse Hero. The power of the stone flowing between you two."

As Hazel spoke I remembered the tickly feeling I'd had when Lily was waving her hand in front of me with the stone in her fist. It made me want to scratch but I knew I'd had to stand still.

While I concentrated on that feeling, Lily began to laugh and cry at the same time. "Oh, Lily, I'm sorry. I didn't mean to make you cry." What and idiot I was!

"No, no. It's ok, Hero. You don't understand. Because of you; because of our bond and the ring you gave me and the shared experience with the stone, I felt a small hum of recognition."

"What? Really? Oh my God! Wait – this is a good thing right?"

This time Hazel laughed. Kin shook his head. I'd deal with that later. "Yes," answered Lily. "It's a very good thing. I didn't think I'd be able to reconnect with any of my stones. And it's incredibly difficult to form bonds with new stones once you are an adult. And now I have a chance of getting at least one of my stones back."

"That's great! But don't you have memories with all of your stones? You must have shared memories with most of them."

"Yes, I do. But you gave me your ring."

"Ok, I think you guys have neglected to tell me something about the ring. It seems to be a bigger deal than I realize."

"Oh, Hero, it's a very big deal. Even though you are not a fae, you sacrificed a stone that had great value to you out of love and friendship. That is one of the greatest gifts someone in our world can give. You humans make jokes and silly romantic gestures about love and what it means, but to us it truly has great power."

I chose to ignore the slur on Human Kind. "My grandmother gave me that ring," I said simply.

"And she loved you so much. I can feel her love in the ring. Just as I can feel your love for her and the love you have for me." Lily grasped my hand and held it tightly.

"You can feel that?"

"Oh, yes. And I can also feel the sadness it gives you to have parted with the ring. That is what make makes your gift all the more extraordinary. It was a sacrifice to give it to me. So all the healing power and energy of this stone is amplified and fortified by all that love and sacrifice. Which means what little magic I have in me is burning brighter and more attuned because of your gift."

I didn't know what to say.

"Do you see, Hero?" Kin asked. "When Lily needed help the most; when she was weak and near death, you didn't just give her your love and friendship, you gave her the benefit of your love for your grandmother and her love for you. And your sacrifice was, well, it was like a bonus."

I nodded. I wasn't completely sure I understood but I didn't want to go around again. The whole thing was making me feel self-conscious and far more noble than I was.

"Well, however it works, I'm glad it's helping." Then I thought, "But what about your travel stone? We used that one together. My first time ever traveling like that was with you."

"Want to try?" Hazel asked Lily.

She shook her head eagerly. Hazel took the stone from the bag and handed it to me. The pale pink stone was smaller than the lapis had been. It was as smooth as glass. I rolled it around in my fingers.

"It's so pretty," I observed.

"Rose quartz," said Lily.

"I was terrified," I laughed at her. "I was so certain I was going to fall, but you just kept telling me to hold on."

I dropped the stone into Lily's hand. "I remember. I wanted to get you out of there before anyone else came and saw us. It had been such a long time since I'd taken a human on their first fae travel. You have to focus twice as hard because the human is usually so afraid."

Once again Lily closed her hands on the stone and once again I clasped my hands around hers. Hazel urged us to remember the stone and using it together. I shut my eyes so tightly my head began to ache, but I thought only about how it had been to travel with Lily that first time. The wind whipping my hair. The feel of the ground disappearing beneath my feet. Her voice telling me to hold on and to trust her. And then Lily gave a tiny gasp.

"Something?" I asked hopefully as my eyes sprung open.

She nodded her head happily. Lily rolled the stone between her hands and then pressed it against her chest. "It is not completely gone."

My eyes welled with tears. Two down. I had no idea how many to go. Twenty? Thirty?

"Do we have any other shared memories with your stones?" I couldn't think of any.

"I don't believe so."

"What about Hazel?"

"It's not the same because…"

"Don't tell me because of the ring. I'm sorry. I'm not trying to diminish the value of the ring and what it means. All I mean is that no one is closer to you or cares more for you than Hazel. If love is so powerful to the fae, then the love you two have for each other has to count for something. There must be some stones in there that have a significant memory for you. Maybe not all, but some. Isn't it worth trying? And if giving something that is a sacrifice makes a bond stronger, why can't she give you something now that is

247

a sacrifice? You are still in great need? You've lost your stones. If the sacrifice is sincere, the power behind it will be the same, won't it?"

Yeah, I was running my mouth off again. But that doesn't mean I wasn't making any sense.

"I can't ask her to do that. Had I known what a sacrifice you were making with your ring I would not have accepted it."

"Really? You wouldn't have taken it?"

Lily shook her head. "I could never ask anyone to make a sacrifice for me."

"But Lily, you didn't ask. That's what makes it a true sacrifice, doesn't it? Because the person who is making it does it out of love and a desire to help. Not because they were asked."

I didn't know if she was going to buy into that, but it was the best I could do. I meant it, don't get me wrong. I just don't think I phrased it very well.

"I'm willing to give it a try," Hazel said. "And I know exactly what I will sacrifice for you, my friend."

"Hazel, no. You can't."

"I most certainly can. Let's get our things and go home to my place. You can stay with me while you get your strength back."

She turned and hugged me. "Thank you, Hero. I don't know if your idea will work, but at least you've given us hope and that's more than we had."

I didn't know what to say. So, I just smiled and said, "Can I help you get ready?"

"Thanks, we'll be fine," Lily answered as she stood and hugged me goodbye.

We all said our goodbyes and promised to call each other soon, and then Kin and I left the faeries to get on with things. I worried whether I had given them too much hope. What if there was no merit to my idea? After all, what did I know about fae magic, or any kind of magic really? I voiced my concerns to Kin as we made our way back downstairs.

"Well, I don't really know much about their magic either. Actually, you probably know as much as I do. They don't let vampires know much about how they do what they do. But no matter what happens, I think it's always good to have hope than not."

"Even if it's false hope?"

"Lily felt something from those two stones she used with you didn't she? That's not going to change. There are a lot of stones in that bag. Odds are good that she'll feel something with at least one other one, I hope. And that's better than she's got right now."

I sighed and felt all the weight of the world in that sigh. I'm not sure why. It just felt that way. Yeah, I knew it wasn't my fault about the stones, but there would always be moments when I would feel that way. And I know I can't be held responsible for whether or not my idea to help Lily and Hazel reconnect to the stones pans out, though I knew I would. Mostly I guess it was because I just felt so frigging helpless and I hated it.

"I'm going to check in with Darius and then I'll take you home, ok?"

"Yes, please." Home. Oh! What a lovely word! Home. Had it missed me as much as I missed it? Put that eyebrow back down. Cut me some slack, I'm allowed to imagine my home missed me. Walk a mile, people.

I selected a chair in the anteroom that was in the least-occupied area. No sense putting myself in the thick of anything. I settled into the not-particularly-comfortable chair and began to think about home. Crap. My business. I was behind, of course. What must my clients think? Ugh! My friends! How many days had I been gone? I wasn't even certain. They were probably going nuts trying to figure out where I was.

My cell phone was long gone. So was my purse. Oh, great. Just what I needed. Massachusetts is not a fun place to try and get a replacement ID. Well, I don't imagine it's 'fun' anyplace, but you have to really jump through hoops in the Bay State. I'd have to cancel all my credit cards and debit card. Get new copies of my health care cards. My head began to throb.

While I massaged me aching temples I heard the familiar clomp of flat-heeled boots on the polished floor. I looked up in time to see Jaeger before he reached Sadir.

"Jaeger!" I called out as I jumped up from my seat. The entire room went deathly still. Yeah, not the most appealing metaphor, but it fit.

The Hunter did not turn his head but I could tell he had shifted his eyes toward me. As had all the other vampires and God knows what kind of beings in the room.

"I- I'm sorry," I stammered. "Forgive me, but it is important that I speak with you." Don't ask me what I wanted to say to him because at that moment all I could think of was that I seriously hoped none of the vampires could hear how hard my heart was hammering in my chest. Would that make them hungry, I wondered?

Ok, Hero. Calm down. Breathe. Still, no one moved. No one spoke. At last I noticed Sadir, the master of non-verbal communication, staring at me intently and then quickly shifting his eyes to the floor in front of Jaeger. After he did this for the third time, I finally realized he was telling me I needed to approach Jaeger.

I bowed my head, mostly because I didn't want to meet the gaze of any of the other beings in the room, but also so they saw me approach Jaeger in what I hoped was a respectful manner.

When I was finally toe to toe with him I apologized again. "I'm very sorry for calling out to you like that. I've been wanting to speak to you but there hasn't been a chance."

He said nothing. Taking that as an invitation to continue, I went on. "I want you to know that I appreciate you and everything you have done for me. I was very worried about you after I was abducted. Even though I was in danger, I was so afraid that you'd been hurt or killed." I said this as quietly as I could, knowing his phenomenal vampire hearing would pick up every syllable.

He stiffened, something I didn't think possible. He had seems so incredibly stiff already. I cleared my throat and tried to remember what it was I had wanted to say. "I um, I wanted you to know, I don't think you let me down or anything at all like that. I don't want you to blame yourself for Aton taking me. Not that you have, because you shouldn't. Just, you know, if you did have any thoughts like that, don't 'cause I know you did everything that could have been done to keep me safe."

Without warning he stormed off and into Darius' office. I didn't know if I'd made things better or worse. I turned to Sadir hoping for some indication.

"Do you need anything, Miss?" he asked politely.

"No, thank you."

I meekly wandered back to my seat and hoped Kin would be out soon. I felt deflated. I just wanted to go home and crawl into bed. Well, I wanted to go home, eat a pack of Ring Dings and then crawl into bed.

Chapter 18

Thirty-seven voice mails on my business phone. Actually, better than I had hoped. And me, being who I am, I couldn't just say, 'Oh great, only thirty-seven'. Oh, no! Not me. As I listened to them all and wrote down all the necessary info, I had to wonder, 'Why only thirty-seven?' I'd like to say my ordeal had left me mentally unbalanced, but I knew this was a condition that had been with me longer than Kin.

I couldn't check the voicemails on my cell phone since I no longer had my cell phone. Pain in the butt! I called the company and made arrangements for a new phone.

Then I checked my emails. Ugh. I wished I hadn't almost as soon as I logged on. Hundreds upon hundreds of emails to sort through.

First things first. I emailed all of my clients, making excuses and basically lying through my teeth about why I hadn't been able to be reached and promising to have their projects done a.s.a.p.

Then I sent out a mass email to my friends. On the ride home, Kin and I had decided to tell them that we had taken a spur of the moment trip and that I had thought I had texted them only to discover my phone was broken and I was getting a new one to replace it.

It wasn't a good cover story, but I couldn't think of a better one. They were still going to be mad, I knew it. They'd ask why I didn't think it was strange that I didn't hear from them. And on top of all the heat I was going to take for that, I'd have to explain why we were going away again right away.

Well, this was my life now, I suppose. Life with a vampire. Life with a vampire? So many things just seem wrong about that sentence. Is it even a sentence? Probably not. Anyway, that is where I'm at and I'm going to have to learn to figure out a way to make it work.

That put me right back where I was before this nightmare began. Planning a cookout so my friends can meet Kin and figuring out a way for them to be together without noticing he is not a normal man.

At least the cookout plans would soften the blow in regards to traveling again so soon. I hoped it would anyway. But, being a big chicken, and not wanting to deal with the backlash from being AWOL the past few days, I ended the email by saying we were on our way out the door now and I'd call them when I came home in a few days.

This wasn't entirely true. Kin and I were spending the night at my house before heading up north, but I just didn't want to be bombarded with calls. I did, however, plan to face the music and call them all when we came back.

Just to be sure, I unplugged all the phones. I know what you're thinking. Coward. Perhaps, but the only reason you might not have done the same thing is because you didn't think of it.

Schlumping into the kitchen, I made my way to the cabinet that held the precious Ring Dings. I nearly cried with delight and relief at the sight of them. They'd never be mad at me for being away. Oh, no. There they were. Dependable. Reliable. Ready to support me whenever I needed them. Bathed in that delectable, non-judgmental, dark chocolate. I took a huge bite out of one as I walked over to the table.

"Feeling better?" Kin asked.

Shrugging, I replied "I will."

"Do you have enough of those in the house?"

"Ha ha. Of course." Ridiculous question really.

"Why'd you unplug the phone?"

I groaned and lay my head on the table. "I didn't want to deal with a barrage of phone calls from everyone demanding to know where I'd been and why didn't I call and how come I didn't realize my phone wasn't working and why didn't I use yours to contact them and blah, blah, blah, blah, blah."

"You're going to have those conversations eventually. Why not get them over with?"

Logic. There he went again with logic. Bastard. "Because in a few days, after being relieved that I'm ok, they will still want answers but will have mellowed. A bit. I hope."

"I hope for your sake you're right."

"Thank you for your support," I snapped as I pushed back the chair in a huff.

"Where are you going?"

"Where I can count on unconditional love and support." I purposefully strode to the cabinet and liberated another pack of Ring Dings. Don't judge me. Besides, I was way behind on my quota of chocolate consumption.

Kin chuckled; but at least he had the decency to chuckle softly.

"You never did tell me what Darius had to say," I reminded him, changing the subject.

"About what?"

I rolled my eyes. "About what? Uh... gee, I don't know? About the attempted coup, the battle? Sound familiar?"

"I thought we went through this? Ilderim maintains he did not cooperate with Aton. And as for those who did, it's going to take a while to figure out who did so willingly and who was coerced."

"But how can they be sure?"

He grimaced.

"And didn't you say that Darius feels that they should have chosen death rather than side with Aton?"

"I'm afraid for most of them it's going to amount to the same thing."

I gasped softly. "You don't mean that Ilderim will put members of his menagerie to death?"

"They're traitors, Hero. Many would argue that Darius is more powerful than Ilderim, and if they'd oppose Darius, what's to stop them trying to overthrow Ilderim?"

"But even if they were forced?"

"If they were forced once, they can be forced again."

"That's awful."

"I agree. But, from a strategic standpoint, I also see where Darius and Ilderim are coming from."

"Kin!"

"I'm sorry, Hero. But we live in a sort of cold war. They have to view things like this from a military perspective."

I was about to protest when a knock on the door interrupted me. "Oh, great! Just what I need."

Seeing as tons of lights were on, no one who knew me would buy that I wasn't home, so it was no good trying to be quiet and wait for them to leave. Steeling myself to take my medicine, I trudged down the hallway to the front door.

Imagine my surprise when the face that greeted me wasn't Sue or Debbie or any of my friends, but Detective Joyce. My old pal from the police.

"You?" I said, not bothering to hide my shock.

"Yeah, I'm real happy to see you too," he answered back with his usual lack of enthusiasm. "So, you're not dead."

"Keen observation."

"Some of your friends made a big stink about you going missing. Where've you been?"

Oh crap. That's just great. They'd filed a Missing Person's Report! "I went away for a few days with my boyfriend. I thought I had texted my friends, but I found out that my cell phone was malfunctioning."

"Is that so?"

"Yup."

"Where'd you go?"

"What's it to you?"

"Listen, I've spent days trying to find you."

"Have you really? Well, awfully sorry to have wasted your time, but I'm home now and everything is fine. It was all a misunderstanding."

He was building himself up for a big blowout when Kin appeared at my shoulder.

"Is there some problem here?"

"Yeah, you the boyfriend?"

"I am."

"Well a lot of people have been looking for your girlfriend here."

"I believe she's already explained that to you."

Joyce grunted. "Where were you two?"

"Why does that matter?"

"That's what I wanted to know," I said.

"Look, as I told your *girlfriend* here," the detective started, pronouncing 'girlfriend' as though it was a dirty word.

"No, you look. We appreciate your coming all the way out here to see that Hero is fine, but as you can see, she is. Now if there is anything else, I would be glad to invite you in to wait while I call your supervisor."

Detective Joyce bristled at that. "There's no reason for that kind of attitude," he said bitterly.

"And there's no reason for you to bother me because my friends got panicky. Again, I'm sorry they wasted your time, but that's not my fault. Thank you for your concern, Detective, but I'm fine."

He looked from me to Kin and back again. Deciding he wasn't going to get anything more he turned on his heels and stalked off.

Leaning against the door after I shut and locked it I laughed. "Oh my God! I can't believe they reported me missing! I'm sorry, I shouldn't laugh. It's not funny, but after everything…. It's all I can do right now. Just laugh."

"Hero?" Kin placed his hand gently between my shoulders.

"And of all the possible policemen to get involved, Detective Joyce draws the short straw!" I really laughed hard at that. "My good pal, Detective Joyce!"

"Hero, I think you need to rest. I'll lock everything up down here." He turned me toward the stairs and gave me a little nudge.

Before I had climbed the third stair, my lightning-fast vampire boyfriend was back by my side. "Can you believe it, Kin? Can you believe they filed a Missing Person's Report?"

"Well, I guess so. You were gone for several days, Hero. It's not such an absurd idea that they might panic and get the police involved. Especially after what happened to your house. Remember, they don't know the whole story there."

Damn! I'd forgotten about that. As far as my friends knew, the maniac who had been lurking in my bushes and had also likely ransacked my house was still at large. No wonder they called the police.

Wow. Ok. Now I really felt like crap. "I'm a terrible friend!" I cried as I plopped myself down on the bed.

"What? Hero, you're an excellent friend."

"No," I sniffled. "I should have called everyone tonight and apologized and instead I unplugged the phones so I wouldn't have to deal with them." Shame engulfed me. I didn't even have the strength to go back down stairs for another shot of Ring Ding.

"You've been through an awful lot. You just want a bit of peace and quiet in your own home to regroup before you have to tackle the next difficult task. That's not so unreasonable."

I knew he was trying to make me feel better, but I was inconsolable. "I could have stood a few calls. I could have."

"Those calls will keep until morning. At this point what's a few hours? Your friends know you're safe now and they can relax and get a good night's sleep knowing you're ok. In a few hours you'll awake feeling better and you'll call them and talk it all out. Everything will be fine."

I drew a deep breath and let it out in a long shuddering sigh. "I guess," I finally agreed, grudgingly.

Kin came and wrapped his arms around me, placing a comforting kiss in the middle of my forehead. "Come on.

Go wash your face and get ready for bed. You'll feel better after a good night's rest. Promise."

I tried to smile but didn't succeed. On the way to the bathroom I grabbed an old blue nightgown. It wasn't very pretty, but it was comfortable and familiar. I needed comfortable and familiar just now.

My toothbrush. Face cream. The old striped hand towels. The scale I avoided as much as possible. All right where I had left them. Nice and normal. I almost got on the scale just for nostalgia's sake. Almost. I wasn't that emotional.

Scrubbed, brushed and changed into my comfy old nightgown I was more than ready for bed. I needed it. No, no. Not 'It'. Didn't you learn anything from the last book? I might kiss and tell, but I don't 'you know what' and tell.

Besides, give me a break, huh? Really! After all I'd been through, being romantic was the farthest thing from my mind. I had been violated more than once by Alex and Bradley in a way that, until recently, I hadn't even known was possible. I'd had my life threatened repeatedly. I had staked two vampires. Yeah, yeah. Technically Kin had to re-stake Aton, but that doesn't mean my initial stake didn't count. It counted, damn it!

Just think about all I'd been through and seen and done since being abducted. Hell, just being abducted in and of itself! You can't tell me you'd feel like getting all naked and vulnerable right now, even with someone as hot as Kin. Oh, you think you might, but as the person who's actually lived through this particular circle of Hell, I'm here to tell you, you wouldn't. You'd want what I want. To just feel safe and secure.

I'll never underestimate the value of feeling safe and secure again. Thankfully, Kin sensed that that was exactly what I needed. He was perfectly content to just hold me close while I slept. He knew there'd be plenty of other opportunities for other things.

"So," he said as we snuggled under the blankets together. "In the morning, you'll make your calls while I pack up the car and then we'll head north. Do you want to go to New Hampshire or Maine or somewhere else?"

"Mmm. Let's just drive and see where we end up."

"Good enough. I know a lot of nice places up north for antiquing."

"Kinley McIntyre!" I said sitting up. "If you're taking me up there to get something on another one of Darius' errands,"

He cut me off. "Whoa! If I was going somewhere specific for Darius would I let you be deciding what state we're going to?"

Freaking logic again. "Mmmm," I grumbled as I slid back beneath the covers. "Fine. But you'd better not be using this trip to scout things for him."

"Look, despite Darius and other things, I am in the antique business and it is my hobby as well as job. I like to go to the shops. If you don't want to go to any we don't have to, but if I suggest any or show any interest it doesn't mean it has anything to do with Darius."

I rolled onto my back so I could look him in the eye. "You'd better be telling the truth. Remember, I've staked a vampire a lot older than you."

His eyes widened. "Er, you had a little help."

"Don't bother me with trivialities! Just remember who you're dealing with, Mister!" I joked as I playfully poked him in the ribs.

He laughed heartily and for the first time all night I felt a little better. "I love you."

"I love you too."

"Hero?"

"Yeah?"

"You're amazing," he said as he kissed the top of my head.

"You know, I'm beginning to think maybe I am."

The Fair Hero Series: Book One – Much Ado About Russian

Hero Fletcher is a single woman with her own graphic design business. On the eve of her thirtieth birthday, Hero meets a tall, dark and handsome stranger while celebrating at a Boston nightclub with her friends. Just what a single girl wants for her birthday!

Kinley McIntyre is not merely a hot guy who has a glamorous job dealing with antiques. Oh no. He just also happens to be a vampire. A vampire that gets his new flame tangled up in a mystery involving an antique Russian snuff box, and a cast of supernatural creatures Hero never knew existed.

Soon her world is turned upside down and inside out. Hero is being stalked by a creepy guy with fangs and an irritating, but ruthless, blonde Amazon. She can't stay in her own home and needs protecting. But what to do when you find out the guy you're dating is just as scary as the people you're already running from?

Before she knows what's hit her, Hero is involved not just with vampires, but with shape shifters and faeries. And as if she doesn't have enough troubles, she unwittingly comes under the scrutiny of the austere vampire Magistrate and makes an enemy of a brutal Hunter. What's a sassy, sharp-witted modern girl to do?

Available at Amazon.com, Barnesandnoble.com, Smashwords.com and www.Fairheroseries.com

About The Author

Kerry Rockwood White is a happily married mother of two who lives on the South Shore of Massachusetts. *Much Ado About Vengeance* is the follow up to her debut, *Much Ado About Russian*. She is also a graphic artist that designs and sells under the name KRW Designs and is particularly known for her faerie and fantasy work. In 2012, Kerry also launched her new interest, Blithe Spirit by KRW Designs; an online shop where she sells hand-crafted purses and hair accessories.

You can connect with the author and fans at:

www.FaceBook.com/FairHeroSeries

Get Official Fair Hero Merchandise at:

www.Zazzle.com/FairHeroSeries

See her artwork at:

www.Zazzle.com/KRWDesigns

See her purses and hair accessories at:

www.BlitheSpiritbyKRW.com

www.ingramcontent.com/pod-product-compliance
Lightning Source LLC
Chambersburg PA
CBHW050019180626
46810CB00002B/488